MURDER SQUAD

BEST EATEN COLD

AND OTHER STORIES

MURDER SQUAD

ANN CLEEVES ■ MARTIN EDWARDS
MARGARET MURPHY ■ STUART PAWSON
CATH STAINCLIFFE

BEST EATEN COLD
AND OTHER STORIES

A MURDER SQUAD ANTHOLOGY

EDITED BY MARTIN EDWARDS

FOREWORD BY BARRY FORSHAW

First published 2011

The Mystery Press, an imprint of The History Press
The Mill, Brimscombe Port
Stroud, Gloucestershire, GL5 2QG
www.thehistorypress.co.uk

British Library Cataloguing in Publication Data.
A catalogue record for this book is available from the British Library.

ISBN 978 0 7524 6300 1

Typesetting and origination by The History Press
Printed in Great Britain

Contents

Foreword by Barry Forshaw		7
Introduction by Martin Edwards		11
The Habit of Silence	Ann Cleeves	13
The People Outside	Martin Edwards	25
Boom!	Cath Staincliffe	47
The Message	Margaret Murphy	59
Best Eaten Cold	Stuart Pawson	78
Basic Skills	Ann Cleeves	100
Laptop	Cath Staincliffe	106
Act of Contrition	Margaret Murphy	120
The Case of the Musical Butler	Martin Edwards	132
Mud	Ann Cleeves	153
Riviera	Cath Staincliffe	164
Sprouts	Stuart Pawson	174
InDex	Martin Edwards	184
Murder Squad: Author Biographies		187

Foreword

Sitting next to a London author (who shall remain nameless) at a dinner recently, I was paid something of a mixed compliment. 'I like you, Barry,' I was told, 'you're a good northern boy – not one of these Southern literary types.' (In fact, the word used was not 'types' but a collective noun referring, I believe, to adherents of autoeroticism.) Sadly, however, I had to disabuse my companion of the notion that I was still a northerner (though I let the word 'boy' ride). I pointed out that I'd spent more years in the dark literary back alleys of London than my twenty or so formative northern years when the Pier Head, the Mersey Ferry and the Liverpool Philharmonic pub were my stomping grounds. However – as they say – once a northerner, always a northerner. And I never feel the truth of this adage more than when I am in the companionable company of members of the Murder Squad (a very civilised group, despite the moniker). This loose conglomeration of northern crime authors actually sport more differences than things in common – and they're a bloody-minded bunch who'll quickly tell you this – *but there* is a shared dark humour, a wry self-deprecation and an outlook on the world that somehow contrives to be both gloomy and cheerful (though perhaps the cheerfulness is a species of gallows humour). In Murder Squad company, I find myself involuntarily undergoing a startling regional transplant; it wouldn't be quite true to say that all my northerness comes rushing back (after all, I still have my long 'a's, unlike the short ones of Martin Edwards and Margaret Murphy), but despite the London veneer I suppose I'm still a Liverpudlian, even though I have a great antipathy to such local icons as the football teams and TV's professional scousers. Writing about and reviewing crime fiction for many years has kept me in touch with *Messieurs et Mesdames* Edwards, Murphy, Cleeves, Pawson and Staincliffe (note the French casually dropped in there — proof of my effete southernisation), and I must confess that (leaving aside their impressive crime-writing credentials) these sanguinary scribes are as stimulating companions as you will find. They are such good company, in fact, that I can even accept the fact that Margaret Murphy will even decline writing commissions ('Too busy,' she says — can you believe it?); or that Martin Edwards has an annoying habit of spotting typos in an impeccable piece one may have written, though he never (well, hardly ever) pins back one's ears on the finer points of law.

However, readers of this anthology will not give a damn about the fact that Cath Staincliffe knows which B&Q sells the cheapest paint stripper, or that Stuart Pawson used to be seen on railway platforms, a small notebook and stub of pencil in hand. Or that Ann Cleeves once wore wellies as an auxiliary coastguard. What counts is the considerable crime fiction expertise of this group, and I can put my hand on my heart and type (with the other hand) the following sentence: the concatenation of talent to be found in this anthology makes the crime lists of many a publisher look (by comparison) impoverished. Reading these provocative, ingenious and sometimes disturbing stories, you will, in fact, be aware of more of those dissimilarities than the congruences between these writers: Ann Cleeves' cool, precise prose contrasts sharply with the more off-kilter psychological approach of Margaret Murphy, while the dark humour of Stuart Pawson is some distance from the stripped-down approach of Martin Edwards.

There is, however, one thing that all the writers in this collection have in common: an awareness of the consequences of crime upon the human psyche — the destructive effects on both those who commit the crimes and those on the receiving end. But if all that sounds a little po-faced, don't worry. The one thing that all the members of the Murder Squad have in common is an unerring grasp of the storyteller's art. There is not a single piece here that will not (within a paragraph or so) have you comprehensively gripped, Ancient Mariner-style. And as to the question of whether or not there is a northern sensibility at work here — well, frankly, it doesn't really matter. Crime fiction has always been — and remains — one of the most universal of genres, and the issues for both displaced northerners like myself and for those writers represented here who still live north of the Watford Gap are, essentially, the same. The matters of life and death so fruitfully explored in these stories are relevant to all of us, whether we are reading them in a coffee house in Islington or its equivalent in Manchester. Having said that, the minute I finished the last story in the collection I felt an irresistible impulse: I found myself booking a ticket to experience again a sensation I've savoured all my life — that moment when the train pulls into Lime Street station, and I step out to the sight of the monolithically brooding St George's Hall and the wonderfully preserved William Brown Street. Did you know Liverpool has more listed buildings than any other British city? Uh oh... getting all northern again; this is an insidious collection.

But if you're in the mood for a trip north, all you really need is the price of this exemplary anthology — which I trust you have already spent. A warning note, though: you'll find the north can be a dangerous place...

Barry Forshaw, 2011
Barry Forshaw is the author of *The Rough Guide to Crime Fiction* and the editor of *British Crime Writing: An Encyclopedia*

Introduction

Murder Squad is a group of crime writers, friends who first met at meetings of the northern chapter of the Crime Writers' Association and who decided to band together to promote their work. The Squad was founded by Margaret Murphy in the spring of 2000. Our first event together was held at a newly opened branch of Borders on the Wirral; we never imagined we would outlive a major chain of bookshops, but part of the appeal of the world of books is that nothing is entirely predictable.

At first there were seven of us, although in recent times John Baker has moved away from the crime genre, while Chaz Brenchley is currently focusing on fantasy and supernatural fiction. But we are not seeking to act out a real-life equivalent of Agatha Christie's *And Then There Were None* – far from it: we have already stayed together rather longer than the Beatles did! Collectively, we have had a great time over the years, occasionally getting together as a group, more often working in duos and trios.

And some wonderful things have happened to us over the years: CWA Dagger awards, television series – the very popular *Vera* and *Blue Murder* for Ann Cleeves and Cath Staincliffe respectively, overseas book deals and countless festival and convention appearances. Margaret had a year as Chair of the CWA, we were featured in a BBC TV programme, *Inside Out*, we have a website managed by Cornwell Internet and we have put together a CD of readings from our work.

This year sees the tenth anniversary of our first anthology of fiction, which was published by Flambard Press, and we decided it was high time we put together another collection. The stories in this book are mostly set in the North of

England, and generally have, in one way or another, revenge as a theme, but they are as varied in style as any crime fan could wish. We hope our readers enjoy them as much as we enjoyed writing them.

I must give a warm word of thanks to Barry Forshaw for his generous Foreword, and to our publishers, for making sure this book has seen the light of day. But above all, I want to express my gratitude to my Murder Squad colleagues for their kindness and companionship over the past eleven years; it is a privilege to be part of the Squad, and I am hugely in their debt.

Martin Edwards, 2011

Ann Cleeves

The Habit of Silence

Newcastle in November, Joe Ashworth thought, is probably the greyest city in the world. Then running up the steps from the Westgate Road he realised that he'd been to this place before. His seven-year-old daughter had violin lessons at school and he'd brought her here for her grade one exam. They'd both been intimidated by the grandeur of the building and the girl's hand had shaken during the scales. Listening at the heavy door of the practice room he'd heard the wobble.

Today there was rain and a gusty wind outside and the sign *Lit and Phil Library open to the public* had blown flat onto the pavement. Taped to the inside door, a small handwritten note said that the library would be closed until further notice. Mixed messages. The exams took place on the ground floor but Joe climbed the stone staircase and felt the same sense of exclusion as when he'd waited below, clutching his daughter's small violin case, making some feeble joke in the hope that she'd relax. Places like this weren't meant for a lad from Ashington, whose family had worked down the pit. When there *were* still pits.

At the turn of the stairs there was an oil painting on the wall. Some worthy Victorian with a stern face and white whiskers. Around the corner a noticeboard promoting future events: book launches, lectures, poetry readings. And on the landing, looking down at him, a tall man dressed in black, black jeans and a black denim shirt. He wore a day's stubble but he still managed to look sophisticated.

'You must be the detective,' the man said. 'They sent me to look out for you. And to turn away members and other visitors. My name's Charles. I found the body.'

It was a southern voice, mellow and musical. Joe took an instant dislike to the man, who lounged over the dark wood banister as if he owned the place.

'Work here, do you?'

It was a simple question but the man seemed to ponder it. 'I'm not a member of staff,' he said. 'But yes, I work here. Every day, actually.'

'You're a volunteer?' Joe was in no mood for games.

'Oh no.' The man gave a lazy smile. 'I'm a poet. Sebastian Charles.' He paused as if he expected Ashworth to recognize the name. Joe continued up the stairs so he stood on the landing too. But still the man was so tall that he had to crick his neck to look up at him.

'And I'm Detective Sergeant Ashworth,' he said. 'Please don't leave the building, Mr Charles. I'll need to talk to you later.' He moved on into the library. The poet turned away from him and stared out of a long window into the street. Already the lamps had been switched on and their gleam reflected on the wet pavements.

Joe's first impression, walking through the security barrier, was of space. There was a high ceiling and within that a glass dome. Around the room a balcony. And everywhere books, from floor to ceiling, with little step-ladders to reach the higher shelves. He stared. He hadn't realised that such a place could exist just over the room where small children scratched out tunes for long-suffering examiners. A young library assistant with pink hair sat behind a counter. Her eyes were as pink as her hair and she snuffled into a paper handkerchief.

'Can I help you?'

The girl hadn't moved her lips and the words came from a small office, through an open door. Inside sat a middle-aged woman half hidden by a pile of files on her desk. She looked fraught and tense. He supposed she'd become a librarian because she'd wanted a quiet life. Now she'd been landed with a body, the chaos of the crime scene investigation and her ordered life had been disrupted. He introduced himself again and went into the office.

'I assume,' she said, 'you want to go downstairs to look at poor Gilbert.'

'Not yet.' As his boss Vera Stanhope always said, the corpse wasn't going anywhere. 'I understand you've locked the door?'

'To the Silence Room? Oh yes.' She gave a smile that made her seem younger and more attractive. 'I suppose we all watch *CSI* these days. We know what we should do.' She gestured him to sit in a chair near by. On her desk, behind the files, stood a photo of two young girls, presumably her daughters. There was no indication of a husband.

'Perhaps you should tell me exactly what happened this morning.' Joe took his seat.

The librarian was about to speak when there were heavy footsteps outside and a wheezing sound that could have been an out of breath hippo. Vera Stanhope appeared in the doorway, blocking out the light. She carried a canvas shopping bag over one shoulder.

'Starting without me, Joe Ashworth?' She seemed not to expect an answer and gave the librarian a little wave. 'Are you alright Cath?'

Joe thought Vera's capacity to surprise him was without limit. This place made him feel ignorant. All those books by writers he didn't know, pictures by artists whose names meant nothing to him. What could Vera Stanhope understand of culture and poetry? She lived in a mucky house in the hills, had few friends and he couldn't ever remember seeing her read a book. Yet here she was greeting the librarian by her first name, wandering down to the other end of the library to pour herself coffee from a flask set there for readers' use, then moving three books from the only other chair in the office so she could sit down.

Vera grinned at him. 'I'm a member of the Lit and Phil pet. The Literary and Philosophical Society Library. Have been for years. My father brought me here to lectures when I was a kid and I liked the place. And the fact that you don't get fined for overdue books. Don't get here as often as I'd like though.' She wafted the coffee mug under his nose. 'Sorry, I should have offered you some.' She turned back to Cath. 'I saw Sebastian outside. You said on the phone that he found the body.'

The librarian nodded. 'He's taken to working in the Silence Room every afternoon. We're delighted of course. It's good publicity for us. I'm sure we've attracted members since he won the T.S. Eliot.'

Vera tapped Joe's shoulder. 'The Eliot's a prize for poetry, sergeant. In case you've never heard of it.'

Joe didn't reply. It wasn't just the smell of old books that was getting up his nose.

Cath frowned. 'You know how Sebastian hates the press,' she said. 'I do hope he won't make a scene.'

'Who else was around?' Joe was determined to move the investigation on. He wanted to be out of this place and into the grey Newcastle afternoon as soon as possible.

'Zoë Wells, the library assistant. You'll have seen her as you came in. And Alec Cole, one of the trustees. Other people were in and out of the building, but just five of us were around all morning.' The librarian paused. 'And now, I suppose, there are only four.'

The Silence Room was reached by more stone steps at the back of the library. This time they were narrow and dark. The servant's exit, Joe thought. It felt like descending into a basement. There was no natural light in the corridor below. The three of them paused and waited for Cath to unlock the heavy door. Inside, the walls were lined by more books. These were old and big, reference texts. Still no windows. Small tables for working had been set between the shelves. The victim sat with his back to them, slumped forward over one of the tables. There was a wound on his head, blood and matted hair.

'Murder weapon?' Vera directed her question to both of them. Then: 'I've been in this room dozens of times, but this is the first time I've ever spoken here. It seems almost sacrilegious. Weird, isn't it, the habit of silence.' She turned to Joe. 'That's the rule. We never speak in here.'

'I wondered if he could have been hit with the book.' Cath nodded towards a huge tome lying on the floor. 'Could that kill someone?'

Vera gave a barking laugh. 'Don't see why not, with enough force behind it. Appropriate eh? Gilbert Wood killed with words.'

'You knew him?' Why am I not surprised? Joe thought.

'Oh our Gilbert was quite famous in his own field. Academic, historian, broadcaster, writer. He's been knocking around this place since I was a bairn and he's turned out a few words in his time.' She turned to Cath. 'What was he working on now?'

'He was researching the library's archives. The Lit and Phil began its life as a museum as well as a library and there's fascinating material on the artefacts that were kept here. Some very weird and wonderful stuff. We thought it might make a book. Another boost to our funds.'

Outside there were quick footsteps and a man in his sixties appeared in the doorway. He was small and neat with highly polished black shoes, a grey suit and a dark tie. Joe thought he looked like an undertaker.

'I was working upstairs,' he said. 'The accounts for the AGM next week. Zoë had to tell me that the police had arrived.' There was a touch of reproach in the voice. He was accustomed to being consulted.

'Please meet Alec Cole.' Cath's words were polite enough but Joe thought she didn't like him. 'He's our honorary treasurer. It's Alec who makes sure we live within our means.'

'A difficult task,' Cole said, 'for any charitable organisation during these benighted times.'

'You knew the deceased?' Joe had expected Vera to take charge of the conversation, but she was still staring at Wood's body, apparently lost in thought.

'Of course I knew him. He was a fellow trustee. We were working together on the restructuring plan.'

Now Vera seemed to wake up. 'What did you make of Gilbert? Got on alright, did you?'

'Of course we got on. He was a charming man. He had plans to make the library more attractive to the public. His research into the archives had thrown up a variety of ideas to bring in a new audience.'

'What sort of ideas?'

'He wanted to develop a history group for young people. History was his passion and he was eager to share it, especially since he retired from the university. He thought we could run field trips to archaeological sites, invite guest lecturers.'

'Aye,' Vera said. 'He tried something like that once before. I remember an outing to Hadrian's Wall. My father thought it would be good for me. It was bloody freezing.'

'It's not so easy to set up field trips these days,' Cath said. 'There are implications. Health and safety. Risk assessment. I wasn't sure it was worth it. Or that we could justify the cost.'

Joe sensed that this was an argument that had played out many times before. He was surprised at Vera allowing the conversation to continue. Today, it seemed, she had no sense of urgency.

'Perhaps we should go upstairs,' he suggested, 'and talk to the other witnesses.'

'Aye,' the inspector said, 'I suppose we should.' But still her attention was fixed on the dead man. It was as if she were fascinated by what she saw. She bent forward so she could see Wood's face without approaching any closer. Then Joe led them away, a small solemn procession, back to the body of the library.

They sat around a large table with the vacuum jug of coffee and a plate of digestive biscuits in the middle. There were six of them now. Sebastian Charles had been called in from the landing and Zoë had emerged from the counter. Joe Ashworth thought she looked hardly more than a child, her face bare of make-up. He saw now that she was tiny, her bones frail as a bird's. The pink hair looked as if she was in fancy dress.

'This is where the old ones sit,' Vera said. 'The retired men and the batty old ladies, chewing the fat and putting the world to rights. Well, I suppose that's what we're doing too. Putting the world to rights. There's something unnatural about having a murderer on the loose.' She looked at them all. 'Who was the last person to see him alive?'

'I saw him at lunchtime,' Zoë said. 'He went out to buy a sandwich, and for a walk, to clear his head, he said. Just for half an hour.'

'What time was that?'

'Between midday and twelve thirty.' Zoë wiped her eyes again. She made no noise, but the tears continued to run down her face. Like a tap with a dodgy washer, Joe thought, only leaking silently. No irritating drips. 'He brought me a piece of cheesecake from the bakery. A gift. He knew it was my favourite.'

'Any advance on twelve thirty?'

Joe found it hard to understand his boss's attitude. She'd known the victim yet there was this strange flippancy, as if the investigation were a sort of game, or a ritual that had to be followed. Perhaps it was this place, all these books. It was easy to think of the murder as just another story.

'We had a brief discussion on the back stairs,' Alec Cole said. 'Just after Gilbert had come back from lunch, I suppose. He was on his way down to the Silence Room to continue his work on the archives. I'd just gone to the gents'. I asked how things were going. He said he'd made a fascinating discovery that would prove the link between one of the early curators of the Lit and Phil Museum and the archaeology of Hadrian's Wall. Esoteric to the rest of us, I suppose, but fascinating to him.'

'Did you notice if anyone else was working in the room?' Vera asked.

'I couldn't see. The door was shut and I was on my way upstairs when Gilbert went in.'

'And if there *were* anyone inside he wouldn't greet Gilbert,' Vera said, 'because of the rule of silence. So you wouldn't hear anything either way.' She paused. 'What about you, Cath? Did you see him?'

'Just first thing when he arrived. He must have passed the office when he went out to lunch and I always have my door open but I didn't notice him. I'm snowed under at the moment and I only left my desk to go to the ladies' or to pour myself a coffee.'

'And then you found him, Sebastian.'

The poet gave a slow, cat-like smile. 'I went down to start work and there he was, just as you saw him. It was a shock, of course, and rather horrible even though I've felt like killing him a few times.'

'You don't seem very shocked!' At last Zoë's tears stopped and now she was angry. 'I don't know how you can sit there and make a joke of it.'

'Not a very good joke, sweetie. And you all know I couldn't stand the man. It would be stupid to pretend otherwise just for the inspector.'

'Why didn't you like him?' For the first time Vera seemed mildly interested.

'He was creepy,' Sebastian said. 'And self-serving. All this work with the archives was about making a name for himself, not raising funds for the library.'

They sat for a moment in silence. They heard the insect buzzing of the central heating system in the background. Joe waited for Vera to comment but again she seemed preoccupied. 'Is the only access to the Silence Room through here?' he asked. Again he felt the need to move things on. The library was very warm and he found the dark wood and the high shelves oppressive. It was as if they were imprisoned by all the words.

'Yes,' Cath said. 'The doors downstairs are locked from our side when the music exams are taking place.'

'So the murderer must be one of you,' Vera said.

She looked slowly round the table. Joe thought again that it was as if she were playing a parlour game, though there was nothing playful in her expression. Usually at the beginning of an investigation she was full of energy and imagination. Now she only seemed sad. It occurred to Joe that the victim would have been just ten years older than her. Perhaps she'd had a teenage crush on him when he'd led her on the field trip to the Roman wall. Perhaps the earlier flippancy had been her way of hiding her grief. Vera continued to speak.

'You'd better tell me now what happened. As I said before, it's unnatural having a murderer on the loose. Let's set the world to rights, eh?'

Nobody spoke.

'Then I'll tell you a story of my own,' she said. 'I'll make my own confession.' She leaned forward so her elbows were on the table. 'I was about twelve,' she said. 'An awkward age and I was an awkward child. Not as big as I am now, but lumpy and clumsy with large feet and a talent for speaking out of turn. My mother died when I was very small and I was brought up by my father, Hector. His passion was collecting: birds' eggs, raptors. Illegal, of course, but he always thought he was above the law. Had a fit when I applied to the police...' Her voice trailed away and she flashed a smile at them. 'But that was much later and perhaps Gilbert had something to do with that too. Gilbert was kind to me. The first adult to take me seriously. He was a PhD student at the university. A geek, I suppose we'd call him now. Passionate about his history. Alec was quite right about that. He listened to me and asked my opinion, more comfortable with a bright kid than with other grown-ups maybe. He bought me little presents.' She looked at Zoë. 'Some things don't change it seems.'

Vera shifted in her seat. Joe saw that they were all engrossed with her story and that they were all waiting for her to continue.

'These days we'd call it grooming,' she said. 'Then we were more innocent. Hector saw nothing wrong with entrusting me to the care of a virtual stranger for days at a time while we scrambled around bits of Roman wall. He couldn't believe, I suppose, that anyone could find me sexually attractive. And to be fair, he assumed that other kids would be there too. At first I revelled in it. The attention. Gilbert had a car and sitting beside him I felt like a princess. He brought a picnic. Cider. My first taste of alcohol. And the arm around my shoulder, the hand on my knee, what harm could there be in that?'

She came to a stop again.

'He sexually assaulted me.' Her voice was suddenly bright and brittle. 'One afternoon in May. Full sunshine and birds singing fit to bust. Skylarks and curlew. We'd climbed onto the moors beyond the wall, to get a proper view of the scale of it, he said. There was nobody about for miles. He spread out a blanket and pulled me down with him. There was a smell of warm grass and sheep shit. I fought back, but he was stronger than me. In the end there was nothing I could do but let him get on with it. Afterwards he cried.' She looked up at them. 'I didn't cry. I wasn't going to give him the satisfaction.'

For a moment Joe was tempted to reach out and touch her hand, but that of course would have been impossible.

'I never told anyone,' Vera said. 'Who would I tell? Hector? A teacher? How could I? I refused to go out with Gilbert again and Hector called me moody and ungrateful. But I should have told. I should have gone to the police. Because the man had committed a crime and the law is all we have to hold things together.'

Vera stood up.

'I don't believe he's changed,' she said. 'He wasn't stopped, you see. He got away with it. My responsibility. We'll find images of children on his computer, no doubt about that.' She turned to Sebastian Charles. 'You were right. He *was* a creepy man.'

She paused for a moment. 'So who killed him?' Her voice became gentle, at least as gentle as a hippo's could be. 'You look like a twelve year old, Zoë. Did he try it on with you?'

'No!' The woman was horrified.

'Of course not. It wasn't a child's body he wanted as much as a child's mind. The need to control and to teach.'

Vera turned again, this time to the middle-aged librarian, who was sitting next to her. 'Why don't you tell us what happened?'

Cath was very upright in her chair. She stared ahead of her. For a moment Joe thought she would refuse to speak. But the words came at last, carefully chosen and telling.

'He befriended Evie, my elder daughter. When my husband left last year she was the person most affected by our separation. She's always been a shy child and she became uncommunicative and withdrawn. Gilbert had been part of our lives since I first took over here. I invited him to family parties and to Sunday lunch. I suppose I felt sorry for him. And I thought it would be good for Evie to have some male influence once Nicholas left. He made history come alive for her with his stories of Roman soldiers and the wild border reivers. On the last day of the October half term he took her out. Like your father, I assumed other children would be present. That was certainly the impression he gave. Like your father, it never occurred to me that she could come to harm with him.'

'He assaulted her,' Vera said.

'She won't tell me exactly what happened. He threatened her, I think. Made her promise to keep secrets. But something happened that afternoon. It's as if she's frozen, a shell of the child she once was. The innocence sucked out of her. I should be grateful, I suppose, that she's alive and that he brought her home to me.' Cath looked at Vera. 'The only thing she did say was that he cried.'

'So you killed him?'

'I went to the Silence Room to talk to him. I knew he was alone there. Zoë was busy on the phone and didn't notice that I left the office. I closed the heavy door behind me and asked him what he'd done to Evie. He put his finger to his lips. "I think you of all people should respect the tradition of the Silence Room," he said in a pompous whisper, barely loud enough for me to hear. I shouted then: "What did you do to my child?"' Telling the story Cath raised her voice so she was shouting again.

She caught her breath for a moment and then she continued: 'Gilbert set down his pen. "Nothing that she didn't want me to do," he said. "And nothing that you'll be able to prove." He was still whispering. Then he started work again. That was when I picked up the book he was reading. That was when I killed him. I left the Silence Room, collected a mug of coffee at the top of the stairs and returned to my office.'

Nobody spoke.

'Oh pet,' Vera said. 'Why didn't you come to me?'

'What would you have done, Vera? Dragged Evie through the courts, forced her to give evidence, to be examined? Don't you think she's been through enough?'

'And now?' Vera cried. 'What will happen to her now?'

Joe sat as still as the rest of them but thoughts were spinning round his mind. What would he have done? *I wouldn't have let my daughter out with a pervert in the first place. I'll never leave my wife.* But he knew that however hard he tried he could never protect his children from all the dangers of the world. And that he'd probably have killed the bastard too. He stood up.

'Catherine Richardson, I'm arresting you for the murder of Gilbert Wood.' It was Vera, pre-empting him. Taking responsibility. Putting the world to rights.

Martin Edwards

The People Outside

The shouting began at midnight.

Ellie turned over in bed, pulling the blanket tight against her chin. Screwing her eyes shut, she prayed they soon would go away. Impossible to sleep in this heat. Even in her thin summer pyjamas, she was sweating under the covers. The weather was to blame, she told herself, it brought out the worst in people. They didn't have enough to occupy their minds. When she was in her teens and early twenties, she and her friends would never have indulged in rowdiness and vandalism. Things were different now, time moved on, but not all change was for the better. People these days lacked respect, they lacked a sense of shame. This was a favourite theme, and it distracted her for several minutes.

But the shouting did not stop.

She refused to strain her ears in an attempt to make out the words. Barry's dogs were barking and the jumble of sounds was impossible to disentangle. Six months earlier she'd invested in a pair of digital hearing aids, so tiny that you scarcely remembered you were wearing them, and nobody else would notice unless they were really looking. Last thing at night, before she climbed into bed, she tucked the little gadgets away into their smart leather carrying case. She wasn't deaf, just hard of hearing, but for years she'd lived in a quiet world. Usually, nothing disturbed her slumber until she woke in the small hours to answer a call of nature.

Tonight her hearing loss was a blessed relief. She would not like to know what the people outside were shouting. Drinking didn't only loosen their tongues, it fouled their language. Even when they were not picking on a helpless victim, they stood around on street corners up and down the council estate, swigging from cans and abusing anyone who had the misfortune to pass by. Ellie had never witnessed this, but she'd heard talk of it in the Centre. Little ones as young as eleven or twelve were out all night, bingeing on drink and drugs, or so her neighbours said. People from the estate hated the residents of Canaan, assuming them to be better off, with a bit of money put away. Canaan was hardly Mayfair, it didn't even compare with the select parts of Colwyn Bay, but more than a fence and a narrow lane that divided it from the estate. Whether the stories she heard in the Centre were true, or embroidered by folk who had too much time on their hands, Ellie was never sure. She was an intelligent woman, well-educated, but now she was out of touch, too old to find it easy to distinguish between knowledge and rumour.

The shouting grew louder. Poor Norman, he'd done nothing to deserve such cruelty. He was a decent fellow who always kept himself tidy. Even though he suffered dreadfully with arthritis, his caravan was spick and span. You could eat your dinner off the floor. He was a private man, kept himself to himself and although their caravans were only a stone's throw apart, Ellie would describe him as an acquaintance rather than a friend. One day, they'd got talking and he confided that he'd spent ten years in the army, though he'd never seen a shot fired in anger. So he wouldn't come out of his caravan with all guns blazing, literally or metaphorically, and that's what it might take to shift the wretched crowd out in the road, hurling abuse and threats. The previous night, they'd given up after ten minutes, but this time the noise was as insistent, as menacing, as rolls of summer thunder.

Glass crashed and Ellie heard boozy cheering. She flinched. One of the youths must have thrown a stone through Norman's window. Why didn't that idle so-and-so Barry do something? His dogs were barking furiously, they sounded beside themselves with rage. For once, Ellie wished they weren't tethered so securely in Barry's back garden.

For all she knew, Barry was scared to show his face, although with those ugly, vicious dogs at his side, surely he had nothing to fear. But what about Jess? Ellie found it impossible to conceive that Jess would ever be afraid of anyone or anything.

All of a sudden, she heard a woman shouting, screaming, making herself heard above the noise of the crowd.

'Go home!'

If Jess was frightened, she gave no hint of it. Ellie disliked the woman, but she couldn't help admiring her courage. The hubbub continued. Never mind drink and drugs, Ellie sensed that the people outside were overdosing on a sense of power. Perhaps nothing and nobody could control them, not even Jess.

'Did you hear what I said?' Jess screeched. 'The police are coming!'

Boos and cat-calls. Ellie heard wood splintering. Had someone wrecked the fence? Might they even attack Jess herself?

'Go home! That's right, go home!'

Slowly, slowly, the racket subsided into an ill-tempered grumble. Ellie heaved her ageing limbs and sat upright in bed. The hooligans were retreating to where they belonged. She closed her eyes and uttered a silent prayer of gratitude.

'Why?' Norman shook his head slowly from side to side. He had a conspicuous bald patch, but what little white hair he had left was neatly trimmed. 'I don't understand.'

He'd been sitting on his own at a corner table in the Canaan Community Centre. In front of him was a cup of tea that he hadn't touched. He'd leaned his walking stick against the table. When Ellie pottered in at her usual time, eleven on the dot, she became aware of a frostiness in the air. A dozen residents of Canaan were in the room, nibbling at digestive biscuits and reading headlines about social security scroungers in the *Daily Express*, but it was as if they'd deliberately chosen seats as far away from Norman's as possible. She didn't understand, either. Surely this was a time to show a united front? The thugs from the estate were a common enemy. All right, at present poor Norman was the target for their bad behaviour, but it could just as easily be somebody else. She could have understood it if people were thanking their lucky stars that they weren't the object of the hooligans' anger, but this silent hostility towards the old man made no sense. He looked as bewildered as he was unhappy and her heart went out to him. She made a point of going up to his table and drawing up a chair. A couple of women glanced at her and pursed their lips as if she were a teenage floosie, intending to chat up a bad hat. Stupid old biddies, Ellie thought, forgetting that she was five years their senior.

'I couldn't hear what they were shouting.'

Norman's leathery cheeks reddened. 'Filth. Utter filth.'

Ellie frowned. 'It's a disgrace.'

'I don't know what I've done to deserve it,' he said, his voice trembling.

Concerned, she leaned over the table. She was afraid he might be about to burst into tears. This was what those wicked people had done to this proud old man. They had stolen his peace of mind.

'They are bullies,' she said. 'Cowards. They like to single out somebody who can't fight back.'

He bowed his head. 'What they were saying about me – it was horrible.'

'You're just an easy target. They think because someone is old and defenceless, they can get away with murder.'

He didn't seem to be listening. 'Why me?' he muttered into the tablecloth.

'They don't like anyone in Canaan. This isn't about you, Norman.'

He looked up and cast a glance across the room. 'Then why is everyone *inside* sending me to Coventry?'

'What do you mean?'

'Even Mrs Billinge didn't acknowledge me when I said hello.'

Ellie blinked. May Billinge was an old lady of eighty-two, sweet-natured to the point of child-like gullibility, who never had a bad word to say about anyone. Not even Jess, whose high-and-mighty attitude and sluttish dress sense provoked muttered disapproval in most of the residents of Canaan.

'There must be some misunderstanding,' she said. 'You're the innocent one.'

'I feel like a bloody criminal.'

'Nonsense!'

Despite himself, he mustered a faint smile. 'That takes me back. Did you tell me you used to be a teacher? When I was a lad, I had a teacher who told me I used to talk nonsense.'

'Have you spoken to Barry?'

'He's about as much use as a wet weekend.'

'It's his job to look after the Park. That includes looking after the residents' health and safety.'

Norman shrugged. 'He doesn't wear the trousers anyhow.'

'Then I'll speak to Jess.'

He took a sip of his drink and pulled a face. 'Stewed.'

'She sorted things out last night.'

'Aye.' He sniffed. 'In the end.'

Canaan Park benefited, as the brochure put it, from a cliff-top location, the northern tip of which overlooked the Irish Sea. The park was home to eighty caravans and a tattered banner over the entrance proclaimed it as *The Promised Land*. On the other side of the fence lay the council estate, a couple of pubs and the scattering of houses that comprised the rest of the village. The Centre was close to the park entrance and included a small launderette, cafeteria and bar. For eighteen months there had been a rumour that the owners planned to add a spa bath and swimming pool. Ellie expected to see pigs flying first.

The place needed money spending on it, she reflected as she trudged back along the path to her caravan. The fence cried out for a lick of paint and several panels were damaged. Canaan had a down-at-heel look, like a pit village after the mines stopped working. It hadn't kept up with the times and the facilities scarcely compared with those at other parks dotted along the coast. Each year the owners put up the service charge, but residents never seemed to have much to show for it. Of course, they could vote with their feet and move elsewhere, but that wasn't as easy as it seemed. If you sold your caravan – *mobile home* was a phrase that Ellie never had much truck with – back to the company, you would only be paid buttons, and finding any other purchaser was next to impossible. Caravans in many parks were just second homes, but most of Canaan's residents lived here all the year round. At least there was a community atmosphere, that meant a lot to Ellie. But now those wicked people spent their nights shouting vile things at Norman. And even May Billinge didn't have a kind word for him.

The sun was blazing down. Wiping a trace of sweat from her wrinkled brow, she asked herself why her fellow residents were being cruel to Norman. She could only assume that such unfairness was borne of fear. Last night the commotion had been loud enough to wake someone living at the other end of the park. Most of the residents were past retirement age, many were nervous or infirm. Perhaps they blamed Norman, thought that somehow he'd brought trouble to Canaan. But he'd lived here for years, he deserved respect. She must talk to Jess, explain the need for everyone to rally round their neighbour.

On the other side of the fence ran the lane, linking the last handful of council semis with the coastal path. Phone wires ran from ugly telegraph poles on either side of the lane. Someone with a pot of yellow emulsion had painted graffiti on the remains of a burned-out car. A few yards away lay a rusting supermarket trolley, although the nearest Tesco was a mile distant. There was always a lot of rubbish in the lane. People reckoned you could find used condoms, syringes and other disgusting stuff if you bothered to look. Ellie preferred not to think about it.

Ahead of her sprawled the Irish Sea, lovely and eternal. She adored the view out over the water and counted herself blessed that, when she woke up each morning and drew her blinds, the first thing she saw was the vast blue expanse, perhaps with a boat or two bobbing up and down in the distance. On one of her all too infrequent visits, her young niece Sara had sighed with pleasure at the sight.

'A view to die for!'

In her own mind, Ellie had decided that she would like to die here. Much better than being left to rot in some ghastly nursing home. Not that she had any intention of dying yet.

Two caravans were perched on the edge of the cliff, a hundred yards (Ellie refused to have anything to do with metres or any other foreign unit of measurement) from the rest of the site. Her own pride and joy, with its colourful window boxes and gaily patterned blinds, formed a triangle with Norman's caravan and the whitewashed cottage – built long before the caravans came to the tip of land known as Canaan – where the Park Manager lived with his wife. And their dogs.

In Ellie's book, things had never been the same since Barry's predecessor, a nice man called Vincent with an even nicer wife known as Mo, had decided to pack in his job six months ago to manage a pub in Lytham St Annes. Rumour had it that the owners weren't sorry to see the back of the couple, since Vincent and Mo were ready and willing to pass on complaints or requests for additional facilities. Barry was a different kettle of fish altogether. As for Jess…

But needs must. Ellie made her way towards the cottage and knocked politely on the door.

'I blame the parents,' Barry said.

They were sitting in his living room, with its splendid view of the sea. Ellie couldn't fault him for hospitality. He'd brewed up as soon as he saw her on his doorstep and had produced packets of fondant fancies and custard creams to accompany their tea. No wonder he was so fat, he was constantly scoffing cake and biscuits. Never mind about spoiling lunch, he said with a conspiratorial smirk. If friends and neighbours couldn't sin together, who could?

Ellie didn't consider Barry or his wife as friends. She didn't think of herself as a snob, but she couldn't forget that the Park Manager was someone whose time (and, presumably, whose sweet tooth) she paid for, out of that increasingly burdensome service charge. Not that it mattered. All she cared about was ensuring that the events of the previous night were never repeated. The trouble was, Barry didn't have anything to offer beyond tea and sympathy.

'The question is,' she said with asperity, 'what will you do if we have the same disgraceful performance tonight? Or on any other night, come to that?'

'Look, Ellie, I'll be honest with you.'

Ellie wrinkled her nose. A man with better manners would have asked her permission before using her first name in such a familiar fashion. Besides, in her experience, people who made a point of telling you they were honest were invariably feckless and unreliable, if not downright deceitful. Sometimes they tried to sell you timeshares in Spain.

'The fact is, nobody likes mob rule…'

'It's dangerous.'

'Well, yes… but some might say Norman only has himself to blame for what's happened over the past couple of nights.'

'What?' In her outrage, Ellie almost choked on her custard cream.

Barry puffed out ruddy cheeks. He might have passed for a well-fed gentleman farmer, had it not been for the fact that as soon as he opened his mouth, you could tell he was no gentleman. 'I'll be blunt, Ellie. Some very nasty stories are doing the rounds.'

'Stories? What about?'

'Norman's behaviour.'

'What on earth are you implying?'

Barry guzzled a fondant fancy. 'I'm not implying anything. All I can tell you is that I've heard tell that he has been behaving – inappropriately.'

'Inappropriately?'

Barry assumed a solemn expression. 'With young boys.'

'*Norman?* Is this some kind of joke? If so, it's in appalling taste. An allegation of that kind is extremely serious. Actionable, I shouldn't wonder.'

Barry sighed. 'I don't know the gory details. This is all third hand, it's…'

'Tittle tattle!' Ellie banged her cup on the side table. 'Baseless innuendo! Vindictive claptrap!'

'I'm sorry, Ellie, but I'm afraid Norman may have one or two skeletons in his cupboard that none of us were aware of.'

'I don't believe a word of it. Who are these boys? I've not seen any young boys coming to his door.'

'With due respect, Ellie, you're not keeping his home under round the clock surveillance, are you?' Barry stroked his stomach, as if wondering whether it could accommodate anything more. 'And besides, I'm not sure that these unsavoury incidents – whatever they consist of – have always taken place at Norman's.'

'But he hardly ever goes out! He's disabled. You've seen for yourself, he can't manage more than a couple of paces without his stick. It's all he can manage to toddle down to the Centre.'

Barry belched. 'I'm not his keeper, Ellie. But if I may say so, neither are you. From what I've heard, we don't know the half of it, where Norman is concerned.'

Ellie's reply was stillborn as the door to the cottage crashed open. At once the house was filled with the barking of Barry's dogs. Jess was screaming at them to shut up, swearing wildly. A tide of anxiety swept through Ellie. She thought of herself as an animal lover, but these dogs were brutes. Pit bull terriers, scowling and savage in demeanour, their tempers roughened by the heatwave. Until the past two nights, she'd consoled herself with the reflection that at least they offered a guarantee of security. No intruder in his right mind would want to make an enemy of those dogs. They presented a terrifying prospect even when safely tethered. But not even their barking had deterred the people outside from tormenting Norman with their vile lies.

And she did believe that they were vile lies. She prided herself on her judgement of character, and could not conceive of having been so mistaken about the man. Even though a small voice in her head whispered: *but you can't really claim that you know him, can you?*

The dogs fell silent and Barry called out, 'We have a visitor.'

His wife strode into the sitting room. 'Those bloody beasts, they nearly took a chunk out of my hand. They'll have to be punished. Nothing to eat for forty-eight hours.'

She smoothed back her chestnut hair. Dyed, of course, but undeniably glamorous. Jess took care of her appearance, Ellie had to give her that. Too much care, actually. The purple nail varnish, glossy lipstick and black eye-liner seemed better suited to a sleazy night club than to Canaan Caravan Park. The woman was forty if she was a day, but dressed as a teenager might. Tight tops and excessively revealing skirts were par for the course. Today she was wearing a pair of faded jeans, but they still clung to her buttocks in a way that Ellie regarded as unseemly. There was a phrase for women like Jess, although it belonged to Ellie's youth, and she hadn't heard it in years. *No better than she ought to be.*

'And how are we today?' Jess's accent always grated with Ellie, a Liverpudlian born and bred. Jess came from Newcastle, and her Geordie accent was broad and uncompromising.

'Fine, thank you.'

Ellie's voice was stiff with ill-concealed resentment. Jess raised her voice and spoke with exaggerated care whenever they had a conversation. As if she pigeon-holed Ellie not only as deaf but also rather stupid. In truth, it was nothing personal. Jess treated every resident more than ten years her senior exactly the same.

Barry cleared his throat. 'I was saying – about Norman.'

Jess grimaced. 'The less said about the way he carries on, the better.'

'I've lived next door to him for years,' Ellie protested. 'He doesn't *carry on* at all.'

'Well, I don't know.' Jess did not actually say *There's none so blind as those who will not see* – but her expression implied it.

'He's a harmless old man!'

'Listen, pet, I understand. And whatever's gone on, we can't condone law-breaking. Or violence towards residents. Why do you think I went out there last night and took them on?'

Even though she hated to be patronised, Ellie was forced to say, 'It was a good job you did. It was brave.'

'All part of the service, pet. But I can't do that every night. He has to see reason. You know what I think?'

'What?'

'He needs to move away.'

'Leave Canaan?' Ellie was horrified. 'It's impossible. Where else would he go? The company only pays a pittance when it buys back our caravans.'

Jess frowned. 'Listen, I'm not suggesting that he leaves the Park. The thing is, where Norman lives, he's exposed. Right next to a fence with broken panels...'

'The owners should get them repaired!'

'And do you think those lads wouldn't break them down again the next night?' Jess retorted. 'That's no solution, pet. No, what Norman needs is a new caravan. There's a pitch on the path that runs up from the main building, you must have seen, it's been vacant for months. Right in the middle of the park. If he moved there, no one from outside could get at him there. I made enquiries of top management yesterday morning, after the rumpus the previous night. They authorised me to offer the move.'

'But what would happen to his own caravan?'

'As a matter of luck, we could sort that for him,' Barry said. 'My own mother's looking to move here. She's not been happy in the flat in Rhyl since Dad died, she'd be willing to offer Norman top whack. Far more than he could get from the company or on the open market. He could switch to a 23 foot caravan – I know it's smaller, but for Heaven's sake, how much space does an old man like Norman need? – and be quids in.'

'He won't agree.'

'But that way, everyone wins,' Jess said. 'Barry's Mum gets to live next door to us and Norman moves somewhere safer, out of range of the hooligans. Obviously, then it's down to him to make his peace with the other residents. But we'd do our best to calm the waters, obviously.'

Barry nodded. 'Tell everyone there's been a terrible misunderstanding.'

'Which makes it all the more disappointing that Norman is digging in his heels,' Jess said. 'He wouldn't agree to a move when I put the idea to him. It's pride, that's all. In fact, I did wonder…'

'Yes?'

'Well, pet, you seem to get on with him better than anyone else. Would you be willing to have a word?'

'I won't hear of it,' Norman said.

'But don't you see?' Ellie was almost pleading, not something that came readily to her. She hated to acknowledge it, but Barry and Jess were at least doing their best to achieve a tolerable solution. Groping for the modish cliché, she said, 'For once in his life, Barry's right. It's a win-win situation.'

Norman drew himself up to his full height. In his prime, he must have been a fine figure of a man. 'That's not the point, Ellie. It's not even the point that those smaller caravans don't give you room to swing a cat. Or that the site is the worst in Canaan – and my goodness, that's saying something.'

'What, then?' But Ellie guessed the answer even before he gave it.

'I can't allow some dirty-minded youngsters to drive me out of my own home. If there's any repetition of that sort of behaviour this evening, I won't leave it to Barry. He's a useless article anyway. I'll call the police myself.'

'And how long do you think it will take them to get here? Last night they never even arrived. Despite promising Jess they would come over. You can't rely on them, they're too busy filling in forms these days.'

They were standing outside the door to Norman's caravan. Through the broken fencing, the lane from the council estate appeared deserted. In the distance, Ellie could see a middle-aged woman with a shopping basket, heading past the burned-out car for one of the semi-detached houses. The boarded-up window on the caravan was the only clue to the previous night's uproar, the only reason not to believe that she'd imagined the whole terrible affair, and that this truly was a haven of undisturbed tranquillity, a promised land. Norman gazed over her shoulder and out to sea before replying.

'You know something, Ellie?'

'Tell me,' she said softly.

'I've always loved it here. Before I came to Canaan, the fact is, I've never lived anywhere beautiful in my entire life. Oh, I know the park is run down and the Centre's like a reception area at a mortuary. But that doesn't matter. I was lucky enough to find a place with a marvellous outlook and whenever I see those breaking waves, my heart lifts. The aches and pains of old age fade away. Am I making sense?'

She nodded. Of course, she felt exactly the same.

'That's your answer, then. I don't want to give this up for a tiny caravan on that tatty pitch at the other end of the park. Even if it is out of shouting range for the people from the estate. I've not done anything wrong, it's all a pack of lies, even if plenty of folk who should know better have been taken in.'

'Not me.'

He nodded and for a brief moment she saw an unexpected tenderness in his faded blue eyes. 'No, not you. Well, I'm not going to run away and hide. That wouldn't just be admitting defeat. It would be like saying they are right, there's no smoke without fire. Any road, I'm happy to take my chances. Never mind about an Englishman's home being his castle. My caravan is my castle. Nobody's going to drive me out of my castle, Ellie. Nobody.'

Jess's face hardened as Ellie explained that she'd failed to convince Norman of the wisdom of moving. 'Well, they say there's no fool like an old fool…'

'Jessica!' Barry was breathing heavily. It was a muggy, uncomfortable afternoon and there were huge sweat stains on his shirt.

'Sorry, but I speak as I find.' Jess shook her head. 'Well, our consciences are clear. So should yours be, Ellie. It's not your fault.'

Ellie said anxiously, 'Norman promised to ring the police the moment there's any sign of trouble.'

'By the time they turn up, it might be too late.'

'You have your dogs.'

'Meaning what, exactly?'

'Only that…perhaps you could scare the children off if they turn up again tonight.'

'You have to be careful with those dogs,' Barry said. 'Especially when Jess starves them. They aren't fluffy poodles, you know. Once they get in the mood for a fight…'

'Of course, you would need to keep them on their leashes.'

'We'll have to wait and see what happens,' Jess said. 'If I were you, Ellie, I'd take a sleeping pill. Just in case.'

'I don't believe in sleeping tablets.'

'It's up to you, pet. All I'm saying, is that if Norman intends to stick it out next door, Barry and I can't be answerable. He's made his bed, he'll have to lie on it.'

That night the shouting began long before midnight. Ellie's habit was to retire early unless there was something worth watching on the box (which was hardly ever, in her opinion), and she was determined not to stay up specially to see if there was any more trouble. That would in itself give the thugs a sort of victory. But it was too hot for sleep.

She dared not speculate what was going through their minds. Was it really possible that Norman had done something shameful with one of their number, and that their revenge, although cruel, was somehow justified? She knew a good deal about vengeance, it was a recurrent theme in the Bible stories she had taught in Religious Studies for thirty years before retiring. And she knew that there were few more powerful human impulses, few that could have such shocking consequences.

She made out a low thud. Something hard thrown against the side of Norman's caravan, she guessed. A brick, perhaps, or a fragment of stone or concrete. Was he phoning for the police? What if his pride prevented it?

Switching on the bedside lamp, she clambered out of bed. Once she'd found her spectacles and re-installed her hearing aids, she put on her dressing gown and slippers. It struck her that she'd had a comfortable enough existence. Ordinary, yes, unremarkable – but seldom troubled. Sometimes she felt lonely, but didn't everyone? She'd never had to endure anything like the agony that Norman must be experiencing right now.

She could hear with uncomfortable precision the terrible things the people outside were shouting. Norman was a stranger to them, and yet they were behaving as if he were a cancer that would destroy the whole of Canaan if not cut out. She knew little about paedophiles, other than what she read in the newspapers, but she found it impossible to believe that a fellow as reserved, as decent as Norman could behave wickedly towards young boys. Of course, she wasn't entirely naïve. She was well aware that wicked men traded on giving the impression that they were kindly and caring in order to win trust. But Norman wasn't like that. The stories could not be true.

A shattering of glass, a series of tearing noises as the remaining panels of the fence were torn asunder. Furious voices, coming nearer, nearer, nearer.

She shuffled to the window and parted the blind a fraction, praying that she would not attract attention. The Park Manager's cottage was in darkness, curtains firmly drawn, but the lamp above the door to Norman's caravan was glowing and there was a light at his window. She saw shadows advancing towards her neighbour's caravan, fifteen people or more. Some of them were wielding weapons – strips of fencing panel, perhaps – like gladiators. But they weren't going into battle, their enemy was a disabled old man who could entertain no hope of defending himself.

She could almost smell the rage of the mob. There was anger in the way they strutted, bent on a vengeance that lacked rhyme or reason. The night was sultry, but she couldn't help shivering. She wrapped the gown tight around her thin shoulders for comfort.

The door of Norman's caravan swung open. She saw him in the doorway, bathed in the bright glow from the lamp. Three steps ran down to the ground; he was standing above his oppressors, hands stretched out, as if in supplication.

His mouth twitched. She couldn't hear what he said, but she could see the anguish etched on his face, she could read his lips.

'Please. *Please*.'

The shadows kept moving. They had scented blood, they were not going to stop. A stone hammered against the side of the caravan, missing Norman's head by inches. Dizzy with fear, Ellie held her breath.

Norman's face creased in anguish and pain. Suddenly he swayed, then pitched head first down the steps.

'A stroke, was it?' May Billinge said. 'Oh dear me, how dreadful.'

Midday in the Centre and there was only one topic of conversation. Norman had died and it seemed to Ellie that the air was heavy with a sulky unhappiness, not quite grief, not quite guilt. Although he'd kept himself to himself, he'd lived at Canaan so long that everyone knew him, if only by sight. Now folk were wondering if they'd been too quick to believe the vicious hearsay. They belonged to a generation that didn't speak ill of the dead. After all, nobody seemed to have come across a shred of evidence to substantiate talk that the old man was some sort of child molester.

'He was frightened to death, if you ask me,' Ellie said.

'Oh dear.' May swallowed. 'How awful.'

'Yes.'

'But the people outside didn't – hurt him, did they? It was – natural causes.'

Ellie sniffed. 'If you ask me, there's nothing natural about hurling abuse at a defenceless old man, or throwing stones at his home, or tearing down a fence.'

'Barry said that by the time help arrived, there was no sign of any of the troublemakers.'

Ellie nodded. After seeing Norman collapse, she must have fainted. She'd fainted a couple of times lately; perhaps her doctor was right to suggest that she was anaemic, although so far she'd never bothered to take her prescription to the chemist. By the time she came round, a police car and an ambulance were parked outside Norman's caravan and Barry and Jess were deep in conversation with a uniformed constable. The lane was deserted, the threatening shadows had disappeared. Feeling old and helpless, Ellie had crept back to bed. There was nothing she could do.

She'd woken half an hour later than usual, drained by the horrors of the night. As she made herself a cup of tea, Barry turned up at her door. While he explained that Norman had died in hospital, she sipped at her drink and said nothing. Her mind whirled with confusion and dismay. He told her that the police were conducting inquiries on the estate, quizzing the people outside to see if they could identify the ringleaders. Though the sergeant had confided in him that they didn't hold out much hope. The people on the outside would stick together. The fence might be down, but the police would run into a wall of silence.

'Makes you question your faith, don't you think?' May said sadly. 'That such a thing can happen in this day and age. Such a pointless waste of life.'

Ellie stared across the table at the faded, anxious face. 'Perhaps not.'

'What do you mean?'

'I'm going to speak to Barry and Jess.'

'Feeling better, then?' Barry asked. 'You looked all in this morning, I'm glad to see a bit of colour's come back to your cheeks. Can I offer you a cup of tea?'

'No, thank you.' For all her anger, Ellie never forgot her manners. They were sitting in the living room of the cottage. The window was open to let in some air and Ellie fancied she could smell the salt of the sea. 'I just wanted a word.'

'It's about Norman?' Jess asked. 'Well, you mustn't distress yourself, dear. He'd reached a ripe old age. He'd had a good innings.'

Ellie glared at the woman. The customary clichés were of scant comfort. But that wasn't the main reason for her quiet fury.

'Do you realise what you've done?'

The couple stared at her. 'What do you mean?' Jess demanded.

'I mean this.' Ellie took a deep breath. 'I want you to know, I hold you responsible for Norman's death.'

Jess's powdered face darkened. 'What on earth are you talking about?'

'None of this made any sense. Not these absurd stories about Norman, not the way the people from the estate have been behaving. None of it. Until May Billinge made me realise what has really happened?'

'May Billinge? But she's…'

'Ga-ga?' Ellie gave a grim smile. 'Not quite. She said that Norman's death was pointless, but actually, his death was extremely convenient for you.'

'That's a wicked thing to say!' Barry exclaimed.

'But true.' Outside the cottage, the dogs started barking. 'You wanted rid of him from next door so that your mother could move in to his caravan. But Norman was settled. He couldn't be tempted. So you decided to force him out.'

Jess gave her a bleak look. 'I hope you don't repeat that accusation outside, Ellie. Not unless you have a very good lawyer.'

'I'll take my chances. Because I'm right, aren't I? You spread a wicked rumour that didn't have a shred of truth in it. You wanted to stoke up anger amongst the people on the estate. You know as well as I do that they can't bear us, they'd latch on to any excuse to make mischief.'

'A load of good-for-nothings.' A faint smile played on Jess's scarlet lips. 'Yobs.'

'And easily led. Or misled.'

'Look here,' Barry said. 'You can't…'

'Hear me out,' Ellie interrupted and Barry subsided like a punctured balloon. 'You didn't call the police at all, did you, Jess? You pretended you'd rung them, but really you were just warning the people outside that they ought to make themselves scarce. You still hoped Norman could be persuaded. You thought you could use me to twist his arm.'

Barry turned to Jess. 'She's lost the plot, hasn't she? She's doolally.'

But Jess wasn't paying attention to him. Her eyes didn't leave Ellie's white, unhappy face. 'If only he'd listened to reason.'

Ellie stood up. 'But people don't always listen to reason, do they? And the people outside won't. Not now you've stirred them up. Do you realise what you've unleashed?'

Jess laughed, a harsh and bitter sound. 'Should I be scared?'

'Yes,' Ellie said. 'You'll come to a bad end.'

'You're rambling, Ellie. If I were you, I'd have a word with your doctor. Perhaps he can prescribe something. Help you settle down.'

The shouting began at ten o'clock. Ellie was in the bedroom, but she was still fully dressed. She'd wondered if the police might leave someone on guard, to make sure there wasn't any trouble. But of course, she kept reading in the paper that the local force was woefully under-manned.

The people outside started banging bricks against dustbin lids in a dull yet forbidding rhythm. Barry's dogs were barking in furious response, but she guessed that they were still tied up in his back yard. She couldn't help being afraid. Even though she was an old woman and, like Norman, she'd had a good innings. That wasn't the point: she wanted to live, as Norman had wanted to live. She owed it to him not to give up without a fight. Whatever the people outside tried to do to her, she would be ready. On her bedside table lay a steak knife and a heavy iron paperweight.

Glass tinkled. Another broken window, but not in her own caravan, thank God. It must belong to the cottage. She couldn't make out what the people outside were chanting. At first the sound reminded her of a football crowd on television, mindless and drunken. But then she realised where she'd heard such a noise before. In a film about an army of infidels, marching into war.

She hurried to the telephone. She'd never dialled 999 before, but she'd never been so afraid before.

The phone line was dead.

Oh, dear God.

Blinking away tears, she stumbled to the window and parted the blind. The telephone line was no longer suspended between the telegraph poles. For a moment she thought she was going to be sick.

She glanced round and saw that tonight the lights were on in the cottage. At an upstairs window, the curtains were parted. Jess was sitting there, arms folded, defiant. Thank goodness. Even if the phones were out of order, she could use her mobile. Of course, Ellie didn't have one.

Suddenly she remembered that when Sara came to visit, she used to complain that her mobile didn't work at this end of the park. She'd had to walk to the Centre to get a signal.

The people from outside were advancing towards the cottage, just as they had advanced towards Norman's caravan the previous night. They were still beating out their cruel tattoo.

But never mind. The front door of the cottage opened and Barry's bulky frame was silhouetted against the light. He had a leash wrapped tightly around his hand and the two pit-bulls were straining to get out of the house and enter the fray. The dogs were barking. Their expressions were wicked. What had Barry said about Jess starving them? He shouted something at the mob that Ellie couldn't catch. It made no difference. The people from outside kept moving. Someone threw a stone and it smacked against the white wall of the cottage.

They blame Barry and Jess for causing the police to come round and start asking questions.

As soon as the thought struck Ellie, she knew she'd guessed right. But what good was guessing right if you were going to die?

Barry seemed to have second thoughts. He slammed the door shut and disappeared from sight. Vicious barking. The dogs had been cheated of the fight they craved.

A stone smacked against the door. The barking grew wilder still. The mob kept chanting. Now they were within touching distance of the cottage door.

Ellie gasped.

Darkness, darkness, darkness.

When Ellie came round, she was in a warm hospital bed. For hours she drifted in and out of consciousness. Eventually, a pretty young nurse told her that when she'd fainted again, she'd hit her head. That was why it throbbed so badly. She'd been out for the count for half a day.

'What happened?'

The nurse smiled, but her eyes were frightened. She didn't answer.

Each time Ellie asked, the staff were evasive. They were protecting her from something. She wondered if she'd hurt herself more seriously than they'd suggested. It was better to know the truth, so she put the question. But she was assured she was going to be as right as rain.

'The people outside. Did they – just go away?'

'Yes,' the nurse said. 'In the end.'

'Did Barry manage to drive them away?'

The nurse scurried out of the ward.

It took hours and a visit from a nice woman police officer to piece together the truth. A truth too terrible to dwell upon.

In the act of bolting his own front door, Barry's over-taxed heart had surrendered. He'd suffered a massive coronary. As he lay dying at the foot of the stairs, it seemed that Jess had come hurrying down. In her haste and horror, she had missed her footing and fallen to the ground. She'd broken not only her leg, but her pelvis. The pain must have been agonising. She could not move.

The dogs were ravenous, they'd gone too long without food. Maddened by the heat and by the uproar from the people outside, they had shown no mercy.

All that Ellie could think of, as her mind spun, was a passage from her teaching days. The story of Naboth's vineyard, a tale so brutal that it became imprinted on her memory. Her lips moved soundlessly as she recalled the stern words that the Lord instructed the prophet to repeat to Ahab:

In the place where dogs licked the blood of Naboth shall the dogs lick thy blood, even thine.

And when the prophet spoke to Ahab's wife, he'd said this:
The dogs shall eat Jezebel.
And so they had.

Boom!

Boom! That's the first thing anyone knows about it. This massive explosion. 20.44. We hear it at the police station three miles away. In minutes we're on full alert, the lines are jammed with 999s and there's rumours flying this way and that: it's a bomb, it's a plane gone down at the airport, it's the Hilton Tower (that's the big one on Deansgate – forty-seven storeys. I wouldn't fancy that, I get dizzy in my high heels. And I can tell for a fact it's nothing to do with the Hilton, even in the dark, I can see it from the window, lit up with coloured lights).

Anyway, my first thought is fireworks. Some muppet importing Black Panther or Red Scorpion or whatever the latest line in illegal Chinese mortars go by and his stock has gone up in flames. Before the new restrictions came in, it sounded like a war zone here, every autumn. Heavy artillery over Ladybarn, sustained bombardment in Collyhurst. Calmer since. Though there's always some bloke willing to risk life, limb and liberty to supply dodgy stuff from late September right through till Christmas.

So, my hunch is fireworks but I'm not saying. I'm a DC, DC Lin Song to be precise, and at my level it's best to be asked before you volunteer anything. We don't know as yet whether there's any loss of life. That's our remit, see: murder, manslaughter, aggravated assault. But soon we get a location and the Boss wants a look and she gives me the nod to come with.

The site of the explosion is a detached house on the Chorlton border, near Longford Park. It's even more detached now. Half the roof's gone and the windows are out, there's wooden blinds broken and tangled. The door's ended up halfway across the street. A car in the driveway is covered in rubble and dust. It's still windy, it's been blowing a gale all day and every so often a gust stirs up the dust and flings it at us. Alarms from nearby properties are shrieking and howling. As well as us, there's a fire engine, two ambulances, bomb disposal, an area car, scene-of-crimes posse, two telly news vans and assorted bystanders. As usual, there's some lively debate between the various services. They've all got a different take on it: the fire officer and the bomb disposal unit want to scope the place out, declare it safe before anyone sets foot; the medics are there to save lives, they want to get in and get people out; the CSIs just want everyone to melt away instead of mucking up the evidence with foam and water and size 11 Doc Marten's.

I'm starving. I wish I'd brought something to eat. There are little flurries of action: the firemen go in and come out, the paramedics get their gear ready to go in. And we get the wink and suit up and follow. They've rigged up some lamps so we can see what's what.

There's one victim. A bloke on the ground in what was the kitchen-cum-living room. Clothes shredded, face cut, blood on the floor. Not moving.

'Got a pulse,' one of the medics shouts. Then it's all action with the oxygen and the stretcher. 'He's been shot,' the guy adds, 'bullet wound in the left shoulder.'

Now that puts a completely different picture on it. Forget Roman Candles and Silver Fountains or a secret bomb factory. Someone's shot the guy then blown his house up. By anyone's reckoning that's attempted murder. We're on.

Back at base the Boss pulls together a team for the enquiry. 'Lin,' she says, 'you shadow me on this.' Brilliant. I want the experience. There's a ripple goes round the incident room: plenty of others would have liked the chance.

DC Barratt's right behind me. 'Tick, tick,' he goes.

I blank him. Best way. He thinks I've got it because the higher-ups can tick two boxes with me: female and ethnic minority. I'm hoping I've got it because I'm keen and I'm reliable and I've got a whole brain.

We establish that the victim is Greg Collins, married to Susie Collins, no children. Now, Susie Collins is an actress. She's been in loads of stuff: *Cold Feet*, *Life on Mars*, *Corrie*. Never had a big part. If there's four friends, she's the one that's making up the numbers, buying the drinks, babysitting. We can't find Susie Collins. Greg Collins is ex-army turned property developer. He's got a scheme going up north of the city centre, Ancoats, near Little Italy. Luxury apartments for young professionals. It's an old glue factory and they've stuck a couple of rotundas on it, filled it with blonde wood and tiles and slapped Juliet balconies outside every window. It's handy for the football, if you follow City. But unlike most of the other refurbishments, it turns out Collins's golden goose has got avian flu. Contractors haven't been paid for the last two months. He's got bridging loans and the planning department have serious concerns. His business partner, one Gavin Henderson, is not best pleased. That gives us a possible motive. A lead. The missing wife is another.

The hospital lets us see him later that night. He's been treated for shock, a perforated eardrum, broken wrist as well as the shoulder wound. They recovered a bullet from his shoulder, likely from a small firearm, and that's with the lab.

When we go in, he's sat up. Bits of gauze covering the cuts on his face, saline drip. He's bigger than he looked lying on the floor and looks younger than his forty years. No grey in his dark hair. Sky-blue eyes, like those contacts you can get. Big nose. Personality wise, I'd say he was taut: one of those blokes who holds himself in check, just this side of angry. Mind you, that could have been his reaction to someone trying to kill him. Keeping a lid on it. And the guy has got military training, that would kick in.

The Boss explains what we know and asks him to tell us what happened. I get my daybook ready to take notes.

'Where's Susie?' he asks.

'We've not been able to contact her,' says the Boss. 'She's not answering her mobile.'

He looks away and his Adam's apple does a lurch.

The Boss asks him again what happened. 'I can't remember,' he says. I can hear the frustration tight in his voice. 'I remember shouting, someone shouting, and that's all.'

It's not uncommon: amnesia after that sort of trauma. The brain trying to protect the soul. In denial. Hey – let's forget it ever happened – that sort of thing.

'Susie,' he says again. 'Where's Susie?'

I slide a look at the Boss. She's not giving anything away but I know she's thinking the same as I am. He's been hurt; his wife's nowhere to be seen. Maybe she was the one doing the shouting. Waving a gun around. Bang, boom. Susie hightails it, leaving hubby for dead. Motive unknown. I don't want to be there when this possibility filters through to Collins.

'How would you describe your marriage?' the Boss asks.

'Good. Why?'

'You've been married eight years. Most marriages have their rough patches.'

'We're okay. No problems.'

So where is she?

'When did you last see your wife?'

There's a moment's pause and a little flare of panic in his eyes. Like he should know the answer to this. Then it comes to him. 'This lunchtime. We ate together.'

'And after that?'

He shakes his head, his lips pressed together. A sheen on those blue eyes. 'Nothing after that.'

The Boss changes the subject, asks him if he can think of anyone who had reason to do this to him.

He says not.

'You're having problems with your business. You might have made enemies there.'

He looks at her, incredulous. 'Killing me isn't going to get anyone their money back.'

Might make them feel better.

'Someone shot you, Mr Collins; it's our job to find out who.'

'Yeah.' He closes his eyes.

'Do you want a nurse?' the Boss checks.

'No.' He opens his eyes. Resigning himself to more of the same.

'The shouting,' she says, 'was it a man, a woman?'

'I don't know.'

'Did anyone call at the house today?'

'I don't remember.' His teeth are clenched and a muscle jumps along his jaw. I'm thinking he wants to scream but he's holding on. Then he says it in bits so we get the message. 'I. Don't. Remember.'

Next stop, Daphne Hart's place. Susie Collins's mother. She has a neat old-fashioned terrace tucked away in Didsbury village. Size of a starter home but they cost a small fortune nowadays. Daphne's lived there all her life. Susie grew up there. Went off to Drama School, signed up with Equity and started off doing commercials for insurance, sofas and frozen foods.

Daphne doesn't look a well woman and even before we say anything her eyes have an edgy expression, flicking here and there. When the Boss tells her the bare facts, she shoots up from her seat, then stands ready to bolt. Sinks down again after a moment.

'Have you seen Susie today?'

'No,' she says, then clears her throat. 'Will Greg be all right?'

'He's not in any danger,' the Boss says.

Not unless someone comes back to finish him off.

'How were they getting on, Susie and Greg? Any problems?'

She hesitates, blinks rapidly a couple of times and licks her lips. Preparing to lie. The Boss steps in. 'There were tensions in the relationship.' Question as statement. Giving her a chance to come clean and say yes.

Daphne Hart nods, casts her eyes down at her hands. 'Susie is seeing someone else.'

'Who?'

'Sammy Gupta. He's a director. They met on *Cotton Town*.'

The Boss looks blank.

'The series about the mills.'

I nod; I know what she's on about. Costume drama it was, bit dull. They used lots of the cobbled streets we've still got.

'Did Greg know?' the Boss asks.

Daphne shakes her head.

'Is Mr Gupta married?'

Another shake.

My stomach rumbles and we can all hear it. I smile by way of apology but it's a million years since I've eaten anything and I'm going to faint soon. Then I'm thinking, if it was Susie who shot him, or the boyfriend, then where would they get a gun from? You've probably heard all that Gunchester stuff and yeah, we have way too many gun-related deaths, but one hundred per cent of that is down to drugs and gangs. Gangs and drugs. It's illiterate nineteen year olds thinking respect comes out of the barrel of a gun, it's lads with more front than sense who know they can make two grand a week doing the business or 150 quid stacking shelves. The guns come with the territory. Small firearms are not generally the weapon of choice for a TV actress or a director. They don't tend to have them hanging around. Nearest weapon to hand for most of us is a knife. Though Collins is ex-army. Could be he's got a gun from his time back then. Maybe Susie or Gupta had got hold of it, or Henderson.

Gavin Henderson is fresh out of the shower when we reach him. Washing away the evidence? Designer house near Wilmslow. He's larger than life, claps his hands together a lot and laughs, breath reeking of whisky, but he's got cold eyes. He bristles when we ask him his whereabouts. A red flush to his neck and cheeks. 'I was at a hospitality do at the Bridgewater Hall,' he says frostily, 'Friend of the Halle.'

Mum and Dad are in bed when I get home. I eat three honey buns and have a big mug of hot chocolate and crawl under the duvet. Not for long enough. My mobile goes off before the alarm. There's a development in the case. A big development. A second victim. Found floating face down in the basin near the Manchester Ship Canal.

Our second victim, Susie Collins. She's drowned. No gunshot wounds. The identification is straightforward, her face familiar to most of us from the telly though the name would be one to fish for.

With Greg Collins shot and half blown-up, nobody is thinking wife Susie's death is accidental. Either she jumped or she was pushed.

'Speculate,' the Boss invites me on the way to the hospital. I'm wondering whether to ask if we can stop for take-out, no breakfast, see, but that might look like lack of focus so I keep quiet about it and speculate instead. 'Susie shoots Collins. Then, can't live with it, chucks herself in the canal. Or someone gets rid of them both: shooting Collins, drowning her.'

'We need to find the boyfriend. And verify Henderson's alibi.'

I make a couple of calls and establish that Gavin Henderson has lied to us. There was no event at the Bridgewater Hall the previous evening.

Collins is dozing when we go to break the news. The Boss lets me do the actual explaining. It's one of the worst parts of the job. He's pale-skinned anyway but by the time I finish he's translucent.

'She couldn't swim,' he says, when I tell him where we found her.

That accounts for the drowning, then.

I ask Collins if the name Sammy Gupta means anything to him. 'No – should it?'

He doesn't need to know, not just yet. It's a judgement call and I reckon he's got enough to deal with for now. I ask him again if there's been any trouble, anything to point us in the right direction. Has Henderson made any threats?

'Don't you think I'd tell you? There's nothing wrong with my memory before yesterday.' He presses his hands over his eyes. Not an easy manoeuvre with a cast on.

'If you think of anything ...' I begin.

'If I *remember* anything,' he says bitterly.

Time to go.

Daphne Hart falls to bits when we tell her. Like her bones have gone. I'm tempted to call a doctor, get the neighbour round and let her be but she's not having it. She's stuff to tell us.

'They rowed,' she says, 'Susie and Greg, yesterday tea-time. Susie rang me in a right state. He'd remortgaged the house without telling her. He was chucking everything they had at bad debts. He'd forged her signature. She was livid.'

'Why didn't you tell us this yesterday?'

'I thought…' she hesitates, gives a big gulp, '…she was so angry, I thought maybe she'd done it. It sounds daft now, but I thought she'd done it and run off. But she's dead—' That starts her crying again.

'Where would she get a gun?' I ask.

'I don't know.'

'Did Susie ever mention Gavin Henderson?'

'Yes. He was taking Greg to court over the business.'

If Henderson has got himself a brief, it doesn't make sense to go round playing Terminator. And why kill Susie?

Plenty of unanswered questions but one ran round the incident room like a rash: any word from forensics? We don't have a lab tucked away in the basement. These days it's all done by the Forensic Science Service. We send them our evidence; they test it and return results. Everything from footwear impressions to DNA testing. They bill us, too. So we have to be picky about what items are likely to be most productive. We're working to a budget. Nothing back yet. There's still a team working at the house and we cough up for some divers to see what else might be in the water: Susie's handbag, for example, or her phone.

We've already ordered records from her mobile network and put in a request for CCTV footage between the Collins' house and the canal.

The Boss wants to see the canal basin so we go out there. It's misty, the sky is a bleary grey and it's freezing. Closer to the canal, we pass the turn-off for Sargasso Wharf. There are big banners slung from the lampposts advertising Food Glorious Food, a Son Et Lumiere with feasting and fireworks. Yesterday's date. Some big bash that's part of the annual Food and Drink Festival. My mouth waters. Sargasso Wharf is ringed with apartment blocks – they'd have a bird's eye view of the festivities.

Further along, where we turn off, you can see what the area was like before. Old sheds and rusting scrap and oil drums. This is where Susie was found. The water looks cold and greasy. The divers are busy and the support team on the side are in ski-jackets and hats with earflaps. I can smell wood smoke. My phone goes. Another bit of information to chuck in the mix: the last call from Susie Collins' mobile was made at 18.40 hours. A few minutes after she'd spoken to her mother. We identify the number. It belongs to Sammy Gupta.

'Boss,' I call over to her, 'we got something.'

Then there's an echo. A call from the steel grey water. 'We got something.' And there's a wetsuit, arm raised with a gun in its hand. Manchester Excalibur.

Fingerprints are basically grease. The weapon's been in the water twenty-four hours but there's a chance. Unless whoever used it wiped it clean. The gun's sent off to the lab. The divers send out for an Indian to celebrate. My stomach growls. We head off. The divers will carry on until it gets dark. 6.30 this time of year.

'Bottom line,' the Boss says as we drive back, 'what have we got?'

I line up the bits of evidence in my head. Shuffle them into some sort of order. Tick them off. 'Greg Collins's finances are in meltdown and his wife is having an affair. When she finds out he's remortgaged their home without her consent they get into an argument. She rings her mother, then her boyfriend. Two hours later, an explosion destroys their home. Greg Collins survives it. He has a gunshot wound. His wife is found drowned at the canal basin and we recover a gun from the water. Boyfriend is still missing. Business partner, Henderson, is lying to us.'

Did Susie shoot Collins then jump, I'm thinking. How did she get to the canal? Where did she get the gun? How did she rig up the explosion? Or was it Gupta?

'Who benefits?' the Boss asks.

'Search me. Though maybe Henderson gets his debts settled with the Collins's life insurance.' We're not far from a pizza place and I wonder if the Boss is hungry but I don't get a chance to ask – it's the divers again. And this time they've got more than a gun.

I wish I had my thermals on while we wait for them to get the winch in place. The basin's deep here and down among the mattresses and shopping trolleys and 150 years worth of industrial gunk is a three-year-old VW Concept – to me and you that's a sports car – complete with driver. Sammy Gupta. Did the tragic lovers drown themselves rather than face the music? Then how come she wasn't in the car with him? The Boss sees me turning blue, either that or she hears my belly rumbling again, and sends me out for chips and lattes. Oh, yes!

It takes forever and an age to get the car out of the water and the body out of the car. The CSIs have to photograph it at every stage and preserve as much of the scene as possible. Soon as I get a look at him, I can tell you what the cause of death is. Bullet wound to the chest. Dead men don't drown and they don't drive cars either. Not even in the wilder parts of our patch.

'Susie shot them both?' the Boss frowns. 'Why both? One or the other, yes. But both?'

I play it in my head. Susie calls Sammy Gupta and he goes round there. There's some sort of scrap and Greg Collins gets shot. Sammy Gupta drives himself and Susie out here. They argue. She shoots him, puts him in the car, pushes it in. Can't live with herself.

'He's a big bloke,' I say. 'Could she lift him?'

'Needs must. But how come no one reported the shot?'

'The food festival. They had fireworks last night. Any shots round here, people would put down to that.'

'Sammy Gupta, then – he shoots Collins. Comes here with Susie. She's upset. Either she jumps or he pushes her in. With two murders on his plate Sammy can't see anyway out. He drives the car up to the edge, puts it in gear, foot on the brake.' She turns to me. 'Rear brakes on a VW Concept?'

Search me. I'm picturing the *Italian Job* with the bus on the cliff edge.

'Anyway,' she says, 'he shoots himself, his foot slips off the brake, in he goes.'

'But he'd have to wind the window down, chuck the gun out and wind it up again.'

'I knew there was something,' she says.

We go back to the office, heads spinning, full of news. DC Barratt's in the lift, all swagger. Gavin Henderson has been eliminated. He lied about the Bridgewater to cover his tracks. He admitted he was at an illegal poker game with some very heavy characters, refused to give details but offered up a taxi ride there and back which checked out.

The incident room is buzzing with excitement. There's been a deluge of faxes and e-mails which have netted us the following: first of all, blood at the Collins' house came from two different men: Greg Collins and Sammy Gupta. Blood at the wharf only came from Collins. Secondly, CCTV footage shows the VW driving in the direction of the canal at 19.15. Next, the explosives expert has identified the nature of the blast: natural gas. An open outlet on the hob was the source of the escape. A small electrical charge from a central heating timer or a light switch would have been adequate to ignite the built-up gas. And to put the lid on it, the only fingerprint on the gun is a match to Susie Collins.

That little lot puts a whole new spin on things. I get it! Like solving Su Doku. I lay it out: 'Susie and Greg argue, she rings her mum and then Sammy Gupta, asks him to come and get her. Greg's not having it, he's losing everything: business, house, wife. He gets out the gun that he's kept since his army days. When Gupta arrives, Greg shoots him. He has to get rid of the body and the VW and keep Susie close by.'

Barratt pipes up then, snide like, 'Why would she hang around, he's just shot her lover?'

'If he's pointing a gun at her…' I say.

'Fair enough.' The Boss nods.

'Collins puts the dead man in the VW, probably gets Susie to drive. At the wharf, Collins puts Gupta in the driving seat. Pushes the car in. At some point, Susie manages to get hold of the gun and fires at Greg. But it's only a shoulder wound, it doesn't put him down. He goes after her and forces her in the water. He walks home, painful but possible. What he doesn't know is there's a pan on the stove, forgotten about in the commotion of Gupta's shooting, but at some stage a door opened or slammed and the wind, fierce that day, blew out the flame. The gas builds while Collins is away at the canal, streaming out to fill the room, to fill the house.'

The gas keeps coming. He's walking back, his mind racing: plane or boat, cash or card? Spain or further afield? Heading straight for an accident waiting to happen. A time-bomb.

Tick tick.

Boom!

He keeps up the victim act even when we tell him we know he's the villain. Even as I read him the caution and charge him. Perhaps he'd have done better on the telly than in property.

Big tick for me, though. And tonight – we're all off for a feast in Chinatown.

The Message

Rules of the game:

> One, find your spot.
> Two, stake your claim.
> Three, warn off all comers.
> Four, wait.

Vincent Connolly is keeping dixie on the corner of Roscoe Street and Mount Pleasant. Roscoe Street isn't much more than an alley; you'd have a job squeezing a car down – which means he can watch without fear of being disturbed. He's half-way between the Antrim and Aachen hotels, keeping an eye on both at once. They're busy, because of the official opening of the second Mersey tunnel tomorrow; the Queen's going to make a speech, thousands are expected to turn out – and the city centre hotels are filling up fast. It's the biggest thing the city has seen since The Beatles' concert at The Empire on their triumphal return from America in 1964. That was seven years ago, when Vincent was only four years old – too young to remember much, except it was November and freezing, and he was wearing short trousers, so his knees felt like two hard lumps of stone. They stood at the traffic lights in Rodney Street, him holding his dad's hand, waiting for the four most famous Liverpudlians to drive past. As the limo slowed to turn the corner, Paul McCartney noticed him and waved. Vincent had got a lot of mileage out of that one little wave. He decided then that he would be rich and famous, like Paul McCartney, and ride in a big limo with his own chauffeur.

Now it's 1971, Vincent is eleven, The Beatles broke up a year ago, T-Rex is the band to watch, and Vincent's new hero is Evel

Knievel. For months, he's had his eye on a Raleigh Chopper in the window of Quinn's in Edge Lane. It's bright orange, it does wheelies, and it's the most beautiful thing Vincent has ever seen.

He doesn't mind working for it. He's never had a newspaper round, or a Saturday job, but he is a grafter. October, he can be found outside the pubs in town, collecting a Penny for the Guy. From Bonfire Night to New Year, he'll team up with a couple of mates, going door-to-door, carol singing. Summertime, he'll scour the streets for pop bottles, turning them in for the threepenny deposit – one-and-a-half pence in new money. Saturdays, in the football season, he'll take himself off to the city's north end to mind cars in the streets around Goodison Park – practically the dark side of the moon, as far as his mates are concerned, but Vincent's entrepreneurial spirit tells him if you want something bad enough, you've got to go where the action is.

He lacks the muscle to claim the prime spots – he's got the scars to prove it – so, for now, he's happy enough working the margins.

The Antrim is the bigger of the two hotels, and he angles himself so he's got a good view. A half hour passes, three lots of tourists arrive – all of them, disappointingly, by taxi. He settles to a game of single ollies in the gutter for a bit, practising long shots with his best marble, just to keep his eye in. It's a warm, sunny June evening, so he doesn't really mind.

Another fifteen minutes, and the traffic heading out of town is lighter; Wednesday, some of the shops close half day. By six, Mount Pleasant is mostly quiet. A bus wheezes up the hill, a few cars pass, left and right, but you can count the minutes by them, now. Things won't pick up again until after tea-time, when the pubs start to fill up. By six-thirty, he's thinking of heading back for his own tea, when he sees a car stop outside the Aachen, off to his right.

One man, on his own. He sits with the engine running while he folds up a map. *Tourist.*

'You're on, Vinnie,' Vincent whispers softly. He picks up his marbles and stuffs them into his pocket.

He's still wearing his school uniform, so he's presentable, but he's pinned an SFX school badge over his own as a disguise. He licks both hands and smoothes them over his head in an attempt to flatten his double crown, then he rubs the grit off the knees of his trousers. Now he's ready, poised on the balls of his feet, waiting for the driver to get out so he can make his play.

In Vincent's book, you can't beat car-minding. It seems nobler than the rest, somehow, and it couldn't be easier – no special props required – you just walk up, say, 'Mind your car, mister?' – and agree your price. Ten new pence is the going rate, but he'll go as low as five, if the owner decides he wants to barter. It's a contract. The unspoken clause – the small print, if you like – is cough up the fee, or you might come back to find your car on bricks.

The man shoves open the door and hoists himself out of the driver's seat. He's not especially tall, it's just that the car he's wedged into is a Morris Minor, a little granny car. Vincent squints into the sun, taking in more details: spots of rust mar the smoke grey paintwork, nibbling at the sills and lower rims of the door. Even the wheel arches are wrecked. He curls his lip in disgust; a heap of tin – hardly even worth crossing the road for.

The man is five-nine or -ten, and spare. Collar length hair – dark brown, maybe – it's hard to tell from twenty-five yards away. He's wearing a leather bomber jacket over an open-necked shirt. He stretches, cricks his neck, left, right, goes round to the car boot, and checks up and down the street, which gets Vincent's spider-sense tingling.

He ducks deeper into the shadow of the alleyway, crouching behind the railings of the corner house. The man lifts out a vinyl suitcase in dirty cream. He sets it down on the road, reaches inside the car boot again, and brings out a small blue carry-all. He looks up and down the hill a second time, opens the driver's door and leans inside. Vincent grips the railing, holding his breath. The man straightens up and – *hey, presto* – the bag is gone.

Still crouched in the shadows, Vincent watches him walk up the steps of the hotel. The front door is open, but he has to ring to gain entry though the vestibule door. Someone answers, the man steps inside, and Vincent sags against the wall. The bricks are cool against his back, but he's sweating. He can't decide if it's fear, or guilt, or excitement, because he's made up his mind to find out what's in that small blue bag.

Taking money off strangers to mind their cars is a bit scally, but breaking into a car is Borstal territory. Not that he hasn't done it before – for sunglasses left on the dashboard, or loose change in the glove compartment – small stuff, in and out in less than a minute. But this isn't small stuff; the way the man had looked around before he ducked inside the car, it had to be something special in that bag. Money, maybe; a big fat wad of crisp new notes. Or stolen jewels: emeralds as green as mossy caves, rubies that glow like communion wine. Vincent sees himself raking his fingers through a mound of gold coins, scooping out emeralds and sapphires and diamonds, buried like shells in sand.

He is about to break cover when the lobby door opens and the man steps out. For a second he stands in the hotel doorway and stares straight across the road, into the shadows of the alleyway. Vincent's heart seizes. He flattens himself against the wall and turns his head, hiding his face.

For a long minute, he shuts his eyes tight and wills the man away. When he dares to look, the man is already heading down the hill, into the westering sun. As he reaches the bend of the road, a shaft of sunlight catches his hair and it flares red for an instant, then he is gone.

Vincent can't take his eyes off the car, almost afraid it will vanish into thin air if he so much as blinks. *Less than a minute*, he tells himself. *That's all it'll take.* But his heart is thudding hard in his chest, and he can't make his legs work. Five minutes. Ten. Fifteen. Because what if the man had forgot his wallet in his hurry? What if he comes back? What if someone is watching from the hotel?

'And what if you're a big girl's blouse, Vincent Connolly?'

The sound of his own voice makes him jump, and he's walking before he even knows it – one moment he's squatting in the shadows, gripping the railings like they will save him from falling, the next, he's at the car, his penknife in his hand.

Close to, the rust is even worse. *Moggy Minor*, he thinks, disgustedly – *one doddering step up from an invalid carriage.* Still... on the plus side, they're easy: the quarter-light catch wears loose with age – and this one's ready for the scrapyard. He pushes gently at the lower corner with the point of the knife blade and it gives. He dips into his pocket for his jemmy. It's made from a cola tin, cut to one inch width, and fashioned into a small hook at one end. The metal is flexible, but strong, and thin enough to fit between the door and the window frame. In an instant, he's flipped the catch, reached in and lifted the door handle.

A Wolseley slows down as he swings the door open. A shaft of fear jolts through him, and he thinks of abandoning the job, but the chance to get his hands on all that money makes him reckless. He turns and waves the driver on with a smile, sees him clock the fake school badge on his blazer and grins even broader. The driver's eyes swivel to the road and he motors on to the traffic lights.

Vincent slides inside the car, closes the door, and keeps his head down. The interior reeks of petrol fumes and cigarettes. The vinyl of the driver's seat is cracked, and greyish stuffing curdles from the seams. He reaches underneath, and comes up empty.

Certain that any second he'll be yanked out feet first, he leans across to the passenger side and feels under the seat. Nothing. Zilch. Zero. Just grit and dust and tufts of cotton. But the passenger seat is in good nick: no cracks or splits in the leatherette. So where has the stuffing come from?

Frowning, he reaches under again, but this time he turns his palm up, pats the underside of the seat. His heart begins to thud pleasantly; he's found something solid. He tugs gently and it drops onto his hand.

He's grinning as he barrels up the steps to his house. Vincent lives in a narrow Georgian terrace in Clarence Street, less than a minute's walk from where the car is parked, but he has run past his own street, left and then left again, crossing Clarence Street a second time, on the look-out for anyone following, before cutting south, down Green Lane, covering four sides of a square to end up back at his house.

The door is on the latch. His mum is cooking lamb stew: summer or winter, you can tell the day of the week by what's cooking; Wednesday is Irish stew. He scoops up the *Liverpool Echo* from the doormat and leaves the carry-all at the foot of the stairs, under his blazer, before sauntering to the kitchen.

'Is that you, Vincent?' his mother glances over her shoulder. 'I thought you were at rehearsals.' His class has been chosen to perform for the Queen.

'We were so good, they let us finish early.'

He must have sounded less than enthusiastic, because she scolded, 'It's a great honour. You'll remember tomorrow for the rest of your life.'

Vincent's mum is a patriotic Irish immigrant. And she says *he's* full of contradictions.

'The *Echo's* full of it,' he says, slapping the newspaper onto the table.

She balances the spoon on the rim of the pot and turns to him. Her face is flushed from the heat of the pot; or maybe it's excitement. She wipes her hands on her apron and picks up the paper. 'Well, go and change out of your school uniform. You can tell Cathy, tea's almost ready. And wash your hands before you come down.'

For once, he doesn't complain.

He tiptoes past his sister's bedroom door and sidles into his room like a burglar. He shuts the door, then slides the carry-all under his bed. He untucks the blankets from his mattress and lets them hang. They are grey army surplus, not made for luxury, and the drop finishes a good three inches clear of the floor. He steps back to the door to inspect his handywork. He can just spy one corner of the bag. He casts about the room and his eyes snag on a pile of laundry his mum has been on at him to fetch downstairs. He smiles. Given the choice between

64

picking up his dirty socks and eating worms, Cathy Connolly would reach for a knife and fork. Smiling to himself, he heaps the ripe-smelling jumble of dirty clothing on top of the bag.

He says hardly a word at the dinner table, evading his mother's questions about the rehearsal by shovelling great spoonfuls of stew into his mouth. All the while, his sister looks at him from under her lashes, with that smirk on her face that says she knows something. He tries to ignore her, gulping down his meal so fast it scalds his throat, pleading homework to get out of washing the dishes.

His mother might be gullible, but she's no pushover.

'You've plenty of time to do your homework *after* you've done the dishes,' she says.

'But Cathy could—'

'It's not Cathy's turn. And she has more homework than you do, but you don't hear your sister whining about doing her fair share.'

Cathy widens her eyes and flutters her eyelashes at him, enjoying her beatification.

He stamps up the stairs twenty minutes later, grumbling to himself under his breath.

'Where were you?'

His heart does a quick skip. Cathy, waiting to pounce on the landing.

'When?'

'Well, I'm not talking about when God was handing out brains, 'cos we both know you were scuffing your shoes at the back of the queue, *that* day.'

He scowls at her, but his sister is armour-plated and his scowls bounce harmlessly off her thick skull.

'Mary Thomas said you went home sick at four.'

'It's none of you business.'

'Is.'

He tries to barge past, but she's got long arms and she is fast on her feet. 'You're a little liar, Vincent Connolly.'

'Am not.'

'Are. How would you know if the dress rehearsal went well? How would *you* know dress rehearsal finished early, when you *missed* the dress rehearsal?' She adds spitefully, 'It's a shame, really. Miss Taggart says you make a *lovely* little dancer.'

He feels the familiar burn of humiliation and outrage at the intrusion. She's *no right* to talk to his class teacher like he's just a little kid. He sees the gleam of triumph in her eyes and hates her for it.

Cathy is fourteen and attends the convent school on Mount Pleasant; she'll be at the big parade, too. But while she gets to keep her dignity, playing the recorder, Vincent is expected to make a tit of himself, prancing about in an animal mask. In an animal mask *in front of the Queen*.

'Get lost, Cathy.'

Cathy pulls a sad face. 'Now Miss Taggart says you won't be able to be in the pageant.'

'You can have my mask, if you like,' he says. 'Be an improvement.' Silly moo doesn't know she's just made his day. He makes a break for his room, and she gives way; it doesn't occur to him that she let him pass. He's thinking he'll buy that Chopper bike with the money in the bag, take his mum shopping, buy her a whole new outfit. He'll get his dad a carton of ciggies – the good ones in the gold packs. As for Cathy, she can whistle. *No* – he thinks, shoving open his bedroom door – *I'll get her a paper bag – a big one to fit over her big fat ugly head. No, a tarantula – no, two tarantulas – no, a whole nest of tarantulas. Six of them – a dozen – big enough to eat a bird in one gulp; evil creatures with bone-crushing jaws and fat bodies and great goggly eyes on stalks. He'll make a cosy den for them under her pillow and stay awake until she comes up to bed –* a whole hour later than him, by the way, cos Cathy's a *big* girl–

He loses the thread of his fantasy. His bed has been carefully remade, the blankets tucked in. The dirty linen he'd used to camouflage the bag is folded neatly at the foot of the bed. And the bag has gone. He feels its absence like a hole in the centre of him.

Horrified, he whirls to face the door, but Cathy has slipped quietly away. Her bedroom door is shut. He boots it open.

Cathy is sitting cross-legged on her bed, the bag in front of her.

'You bloody–'

'Thief?' she says, in that pert way that drives him crackers. 'Takes one to know one, doesn't it, Vincent?'

'You give it back!'

She puts a finger to her lips and cocks her head. The front door slams. It's Dad. She whispers, 'Anybody home?'

Their father's voice booms out, a second after, like an echo in reverse: 'Anybody home?'

Her eyes sparkle with malicious good humour. 'What would Dad say if he knew you'd been thieving?'

Vincent clenches his fists, tears of impotent rage pricking his eyes. He considers rushing her, but Dad would hear and come to investigate.

'Give me it. It's mine.'

'Now, Vincent, we both know that's not true.' She plucks at the zip and he wants to fling himself at her, to claw it from her grasp.

She shouts, 'Is that you, Dad?' putting on her girly voice just for him.

Their father's footsteps clump up the stairs. 'How's my girl?' he says.

'Just getting changed.' She raises her eyebrows, and reluctantly, Vincent back-heels the door shut.

Their father passes her door and they hear a heavy sigh as he slumps onto the bed to take off his shoes.

Cathy is smiling as she unzips the bag, and Vincent wants to kill her.

First, she looks blank, then puzzled, then worried.

'You can turn off the big act,' he whispers furiously.

Only she doesn't look like she's acting. And when she finally turns her face to him, her expression is one of sick horror.

'Oh, Vincent,' she whispers.

His stomach flips. The anticipated wealth – the bundles of cash, the glittering treasures of his imagination – all crumble to dust.

Carefully, reverently, she lifts a bible and a set of rosary beads out of the bag. The beads are dark, solid wood; a serious rosary, a man's rosary. She holds it up so the silver crucifix swings, and he stares at it, almost hypnotised.

She reaches into the carry-all again, and brings out a small package, wrapped in brown paper. Three words are printed in neat block capitals on the front of it: 'FOR FATHER O'BRIEN'.

They stare at it for a long moment.

'Vinnie, you robbed a priest.'

'He *isn't*,'Vincent whispers, his voice hoarse. He feels sweat break out on his forehead.

Wordlessly, she holds up the rosary, the Jersusalem Bible.

'He *can't* be – he was wearing *normal clothes*.'

'Shh!' She looks past him to the bedroom door, and he realises he had been shouting. They hold their breath, listening for their father. There's no sound, and after a moment she whispers: 'He might be on his holidays.'

'He was wearing a *leather jacket*, Cath.'

She looks into his face, absorbing the information, but her eyes stray again to the parcel, as if pulled by a magnet. 'So, maybe it's his brother, or a friend. It doesn't *matter* Vinnie: that parcel is addressed to Father O'Brien. There's no getting away from it – you robbed a priest.' She bites her lip. 'And that's a mortal sin.'

Cathy is in the Legion of Mary, and she's been on two retreats with the sisters of Notre Dame. She always got an A in Religious Education – so if Cathy says it's a mortal sin, he knows for sure that the Devil is already stoking the fires of hell, chucking on extra coals, ready to roast him.

'I'll go to confession, I'll do penance – I'll do a novena,' he gabbles, trying to think of something that will appease. 'I'll do the Nine First Fridays–'

The shocked look on his sister's face makes him stop. But the Nine First Fridays are the most powerful prayer he knows: a special devotion to the Sacred Heart, getting up at six o'clock on the first Friday each month for nine solid months to attend early mass and receive the Holy Eucharist – surely that will wipe his sin away?

'Vincent,' she says, gently, 'There's no penance for a mortal sin – and you can't receive Holy Communion with a big black stain on your soul: it would be like inviting Jesus into your home with the devil sitting by the fire in your favourite armchair.'

When he was little, Vincent's mum and dad both had to work, and Cathy would take care of him after school, in the holidays – even weekends, if Mum got the chance of overtime. Between the ages of five and eight, Cathy had been his minder, his teacher, his best mate, the maker-up of games and adventures. But he'd got bigger, and by his ninth birthday he wanted his independence. He became rebellious, and she was offended and hurt and that made her superior and sarcastic. Now, feeling the Devil squatting deep inside him, chiselling away at his soot-blackened soul, he feels small again, frightened and lost, and he wishes she would take charge.

'What'm I gonna do, Cath?'

She stares at the neat brown package as if it's radioactive.

'Vinnie...' She frowns, distracted, like she's doing a difficult sum in her head. 'There's only one way to get let off a mortal sin.' She turns her eyes on him, and they are so filled with fear that Vincent is seized by a terrible dread.

'What d'you mean, "it's gone"?'

The man in the leather jacket is standing in a phonebox, opposite the clock tower of the university's Victoria Building. The quarter chimes have sounded and the clock's gilt hands read six thirty-two; he should be in position by now. He closes his eyes. 'Gone, vanished. Stolen.'

'You lost it.' His unit commander's voice is hard, nasal, contemptuous.

'I thought it would be safe in the car.'

'Oh, well, that's all right then – anyone can make a mistake.'

'It was well hidden.'

'Not that well, eh?'

The man fixes his gaze on the gleaming face of the clock, willing the hands to move, but the silence seems to last an eternity.

'When?'

'Sometime between six last night and five this morning.'

'*Twelve hours* you left it?'

'Wouldn't it draw attention if I checked the damn thing every five minutes?'

'Watch your tone.'

The man grips the phone receiver hard. The sun has been up since four-thirty and the temperature in the glass box must be eighty degrees, but he daren't ease the door open for air.

'Is it set to go?'

'It's on a twenty-four-hour timer, like you said. It'll trigger automatically at three this afternoon.' He takes a breath to speak again, but the voice on the line interrupts:

'Shut up – I'm thinking.'

He waits in obedient silence.

'Whoever took it must've dumped it, otherwise you'd be locked up in a police cell by now.'

'That's what I–'

'I'm speaking, here.'

He clamps his mouth shut so fast he bites his tongue.

'Even so, you'd better not go back to the hotel. Leave the car, catch a bus to Manchester. I'll have someone pick you up.'

'I have a weapon. I could still complete my mission.'

'And how close d'you think you'd get?'

'I could mingle with the crowd. They won't even see me.'

A snort of derision. 'You've a whiff of the zealot about you, lad. They'll sniff you out in a heartbeat, so they will – be all over you like flies on shit.' The man listened to the metallic harshness of the voice, his eyes closed. 'This's what you get when you send a *dalta* to do a soldier's job.'

That stings – he's no raw recruit. 'Haven't I proved myself a dozen times?'

'Not this time, son – and this is the one that counts.'

'It's a setback – I'll make up for it.'

'You will. But not in Liverpool; not today.'

'Look, I checked it out – the approach roads are closed, but there's a bridge–'

'What d'you think you'll hit with a thirty-eight calibre service revolver from a bloody bridge?'

He wants to say he's been practising – that he can hit a can from thirty yards, but that would sound childish – a tin can isn't a moving target, and it takes more than a steady hand to look another human being in the face and fire a bullet into them. So he says nothing.

'No,' his superior says. 'No. They'd catch you. And make no mistake – they would shoot you like a dog.'

'I don't care.'

'Only fools want to be martyrs, son. And even if *you* don't care, *I* do. I care that we've spent money on equipment and you let a scouse scallywag walk away with it. I *care* that security will be stepped up for every official visit after today – even if you walk away right now. Because there's the small matter of a package that will turn up at three p.m.' He sighed angrily. 'We'll just have to pray to God the thieving bastard left it somewhere useful, like the city centre.'

He books his ticket for one o'clock and walks down to the docks to clear his head. They are still adding the finishing touches to the stands when he stops by the tunnel approach on his way back to the coach station. He joins a group of kids gawping through the wire mesh at the chippies hammering the final nails in the platform. He can see the plaque above the tunnel, draped in blue cloth. This is where the Queen will make her speech. A team of men are sweeping the road leading to the tunnel entrance and a dozen more are raking smooth the bare soil of the verges.

Attendance is by invitation only, but a man dressed in overalls and looking like he has a job to do might pass unchallenged and find a good spot under the stands. Only what would be the point? Without the device, it would be hopeless: even if he did manage to remain undiscovered, he would have to abandon his hiding place, walk out in front of thousands of people, place himself close enough to aim his pistol and fire.

Police are already clustered in threes and fours along the newly metalled road; there will be sharpshooters along the route – and true enough, they would shoot him like a dog.

Father O'Brien hadn't been anyone important. He didn't have the ear of the bishop and he wasn't destined for Rome; he hadn't a scholarly brain nor a Jesuit's mind to play the kind of politics it would take to elevate him above parish priest.

But he was a good man. He came from the fertile chalklands of Wexford, around Bantry Bay, where they spoke in softer tones, and faces were more given to smile. He liked a drink, and would stand you a pint if he fell into conversation with you at the Crown Bar, but he wouldn't hesitate to tell a man when he'd had enough, and he'd tipped more than one out onto the street before he'd drunk his fill. The man's father and the priest had come to blows over that; he'd taken to drinking after he lost his job on the shipyard. Father O'Brien had kicked his da out of that bar every night for a fortnight, until on the last day, his da got murderous mad. He swung wildly at Father O'Brien, out on the street, but the priest ducked and dodged, light on his feet, deflecting and blocking, until at last, dizzy and exhausted, his da had sunk to the pavement and wept.

'Ten thousand men work at the Belfast shipyard, Father,' he'd said, his words sloshing out of his mouth. 'And just four hundred Catholics among them. You've a good education: can you tell me what makes a Protestant better at lugging sacks of grain than a Catholic? Is there some calculation that adds up the worth of a man and subtracts a measure of humanity because he was born a Catholic?'

Father O'Brien didn't have an answer, but he sat with the boy's father on the kerb, until he'd raged and wept the anger out of him, and then the priest walked him home. He knew this to be the gods-honest truth, for the man had seen it with his own eyes, as a boy of fourteen.

Father O'Brien didn't preach taking up arms against the oppressor. He wasn't affiliated to the IRA, nor even Sinn Féin. 'My only affiliation,' he would say, 'is to God Almighty; my only obligation is to my flock.' Which was how he came to die. Not in a hail of bullets, but in the stupidest, most pointless way imaginable. A macho squaddie – a bad driver trying to impress his oppos – lost control of his vehicle turning a corner. Father O'Brien had been visiting a house in the next street, delivering the last sacraments to an old man dying of the cancer. The armoured vehicle skidded, clipped the opposite kerb, spun one hundred-and-eighty degrees, and smashed into the end of a terrace decorated with a painting of the Irish tricolour. Father O'Brien was pinned against the wall and died instantly.

He had been a gentle man, and a modest one, yet the violence and futility of his death had made a spectacle of him: a thing to point to as evidence of the British Army's lack of respect; a dread event for old men to sigh and shake their heads over; a lurid tale for children to whisper in the playground, of the priest who was cut in half by an armoured car. Father O'Brien was no longer remembered for the good he'd done in life – only for the notoriety of his death.

The man had meant to deliver a message: that Father O'Brien's death would not go unpunished, and in failing in his mission he had failed Father O'Brien.

Vincent and Cathy stand in the porch. It's just shy of seven o'clock, and the sun is shining hot through the top light of the front door. Cathy's face is pale.

'You know what you have to do?'

He nods, but he has a lump in his throat as big as a bottle-washer ollie, so he can't speak.

She straightens his tie and combs her fingers through his hair, staring solemnly down at him. He doesn't squirm; in truth, he wouldn't complain if she took him by the hand and walked with him down the street in broad daylight, because he does not want to do this alone.

She seems taller, today. Grown up.

'I'll tell Mum you had to go early to rehearsals.'

He frowns, wishing he hadn't skipped rehearsals the day before, thinks that dancing in an animal mask seems small humiliation, compared with what he has to do now.

'I'll tell Miss Taggart you've got a tummy bug, in case it takes a while, so you'll have to make yourself scarce for the rest of the day. All right?'

He nods again.

She hands him the small blue carry-all and blinks tears from her eyes.

He hefts the bag and squares his shoulders, setting off down the street like a soldier off to war.

The car is parked outside the hotel, but he waits an hour, and still the man hasn't come out. Another half hour, and the manager appears on the doorstep.

'What're you up to?' he asks.

'Is the man here – the one that owns the Morris Minor?'

The manager is broad faced, with small eyes. He jams his hands in his trouser pockets and says, 'What's it to you?'

He's wearing grey flannel trousers and a matching waistcoat to hide his soft belly; Vincent reckons he could easy out-run him, but his great sin burns his soul like acid, so he stills his itchy feet, and composes his face into an approximation of innocence.

'Got something for him.'

The manager lifts his chin. 'That it?' He holds a hand out for the bag. 'I'll make sure he gets it.'

Vincent tightens his grip on the carry-all and takes a step back. 'Is he in?'

'Went out early,' the man says. 'Missed his breakfast.'

'I'll wait.'

'Not here, you won't – you're making my guests nervous, loitering outside.'

'You can't stop me. It's a free country.' He feels a pang of guilt: he promised Cathy he'd mind his manners.

'We'll see what the police've got to say about that.' The man narrows his eyes. 'Anyway, shouldn't you be in school?' His small eyes fasten on Vincent's blazer pocket. He's forgotten to pin the SFX badge over the real one. He clamps his hand over his pocket and the man comes at him, pitching forwards as he comes down the steps. Vincent turns and flees.

He pelts up the hill and cuts right into Rodney Street, then dodges left into the Scotch Churchyard, and ducks behind one of the gravestones, hugging the bag close to his chest. He can't stop shaking. The gardens of the convent back onto the graveyard; he'll catch his sister in the grounds during break. He checks his watch – playtime won't be for another hour-and-a-half. He sits down behind McKenzie's pyramid to wait.

He would have gone – in fact, he was already on his way. If the bus hadn't been diverted. If the driver hadn't turned down Shaw Street. If the new route hadn't taken them through Everton. If he'd looked out of the window to his left, rather than his right.

If, if, if... He would have stayed on the bus and been picked up in Manchester and made his ignominious way home. But in Everton, Orange Lodge and Catholic sectarianism was as strong as on any street in Belfast. A long stretch of grey wall ran beneath the new high-rise blocks on Netherfield Road. If he had turned away, just for a second, bored by the monotony of grey concrete and dusty pavements... But something had caught his eye; he glanced right and had seen the insult, daubed in orange paint on a grey wall – ill-spelt, angry, hateful: 'THE POPE IS A BASTERD'.

He recoiled like he'd been spat at. All morning, a rage had smouldered, built from the tinder of grief and loss, fuelled by the shock of finding the device gone and, yes, by the mortification he had suffered in telling his commander. Now it sparked and flared, and he blazed with righteous fire.

He lurched from his seat to the front. 'Stop the bus,' he said.

The driver didn't even take his eyes off the road. 'It's not a request service, Paddy, lad.'

'Oh, good – 'cos this is not a request.'

The driver swivelled his head to look at him. 'And who d'you think you are?'

The man took hold of the driver's seatback and leaned in, allowing his leather jacket to fall open just enough to show the revolver tucked in his belt. 'I'm the Angel of Death, son.'

It's four minutes to three as he heads south west down Birkenhead Road on the other side of the Mersey. He'd crossed the great wide dock of East Float and crossed it again, tracking over every one of the Four Bridges, lost. Forty-five minutes later, he'd fetched up at the Seacombe Ferry terminal, with just a handrail between him and the muddy waters of the Mersey. He could happily have thrown himself in, had a kindly ferryman not asked him if he was off to the parade, and given him clear directions to Wheatland Lane, where he might stand on the bridge and wave to the Queen. He barrels along, the little car's engine screaming, past a stretch of blasted landscape. His heart is beating like an Orange Man's Lambeg. It's two minutes before the hour. She'll give her speech on the Liverpool side, then motor through to Wallasey; giving him time to find a spot. He *will* deliver the message for Father O'Brien. He almost misses the sharp turn westward and wrestles the wheel right. The gun slides in his lap, and he catches it, tucking it firmly in his waistband.

He's driving full into the afternoon sun, now; it scorches his face, burning through the windscreen, and he yanks the visor down. A sheet of paper flutters onto the dashboard. His foot hard on the pedal, he picks it up, squints at it as he powers towards the bridge.

It's a note, written on lined paper, in a child's neat handwriting:

Dear Mister,

    I came to see you at the hotel but you weren't there. I wanted to say to your face that I am truly sorry I stole Father O'Brien's present. My sister says it's a Mortal Sin to steal from a Priest. I waited for ages, but the manager told me to push off, and he would of got me arrested if I didn't so I couldn't stay. My sister said it would be O.K. if I wrote you a message instead. So I hope you will forgive me and ask Father to forgive me as well. I never opened it or nothing, so I hope it will be O.K. and that you will forgive me.

Sorry.

PS – I put it back ~~esac~~ exacly like I found it.

His eyes widen. He hits the brakes. The car skids, turning ninety degrees, sliding sideways along the empty road. He reaches for the door, but his fingers seem too big, too clumsy to work the handle, he can't seem to get a grip of the lever. He can't seem to–

The thin, electronic beep of the electronic clock in the bag under his seat sounds a fraction of a second before the flash. Then the windows shatter and the grey bodywork blows apart like a tin can on a bonfire.

Stuart Pawson

Best Eaten Cold

If Jessica Fullerton was the Queen of Short Story Writers, Artemesia Jones was the Two of Clubs. Which was strange, because in many ways their lives had run on parallel tracks. Both came from genteel, middle-class backgrounds: Jessica's father was a sea captain on the Hull-Rotterdam run, who sent her presents from far-off places, filling her head with fantasies about Arabian white-slave traders, Japanese concubines and stolen kisses on storm-washed decks. Artemesia's was a pharmacist with a love of opera whose ambition was that his daughter would become an accomplished musician, despite the fact that she had a voice like a foghorn and the coordination of a new-born gnu.

Both girls were unhappy as children and learned to live in their own private worlds. Both went to finishing school – Jessica to Chamonix in Switzerland, Artemesia to Igls in Austria – and, appropriately, lost their virginity there. Jessica courtesy of a visiting lecturer in his hotel room; Artemesia to the boy who delivered the bread every morning, who said he was a ski instructor in winter. Both found the experience disappointingly unpleasant.

Jessica married at twenty-one and was widowed twenty-six childless years later. Artemesia was a year older when she wed a boy she met at Midnight Mass one Christmas, but they were divorced within two years on the grounds of incompatibility. Both women started writing shortly after marriage, searching for romance between the pages as a substitute for that lacking between the sheets, but here their respective lives diverged sharply. Jessica's first attempt at publication was met with a rejection but editorial encouragement, and her second attempt found its way into the pages of *Woman's Own*. It was the start of a rewarding career in financial terms, if not totally satisfying emotionally, but she was content with that. The stories came off her typewriter, and later her word processor, like labels for tins of beans moving round a conveyor belt. She employed an agent and a secretary, and moved to the Isle of Man to escape the clutches of the Inland Revenue.

Artemesia had one hundred and eight rejection notices before a small piece she wrote about corn dollies was printed in the *Dalesman*. This re-fired her enthusiasm, gave her a track record with which to woo editors, and another twenty rejections later she was rewarded by having a story about a lighthouse keeper's daughter who falls in love with a one-legged lobster-potter published in *My Weekly*. In the years since then she'd had sporadic success: not enough to earn her any fame or money; just enough to keep the fires of ambition smouldering and for her to put the magic word 'writer' on any document that asked for her occupation. Fortunately her father had left her well provided for, so she was able to maintain the literary lifestyle: the home in Ilkley (Cliffhanger Cottage); two pedigree Persian cats (Charlotte and Emily, although one of them was a neutered male) and attendance at writers' conferences, symposia and master classes at short intervals throughout the year.

Artemesia Jones knew all about Jessica Fullerton. She had never spoken directly to her in private but had attended numerous functions where Jessica had been a guest of honour, and once even had the temerity to ask a question after a talk on how to defeat writers' block. The answer was etched forever in Artemesia's brain: 'If you love to write, that is all you need. We owe it to our readers to each tap into our private muse and share the results with them.' She was familiar with Jessica's work, too. It was hard to avoid it. Her short stories were regular features on Radio 4 and every woman's magazine in publication. 'Jessica's latest' across the front cover of a certain style of magazine guaranteed a boost in sales. Every six months a new anthology of her work came out and she was a regular contributor to other collections. The bulk of her output was sentimental, predictable, adjective-laden tripe, but it sold like bagels in city coffee shops. Queen of the Short Story Writers was a title that rested easily on her ample shoulders.

So, at a quarter to four one rainy Monday afternoon shortly after the turn of the millennium, Artemesia found herself tuning in to Radio 4 to hear the first of a much-trailed short season of Jessica Fullerton stories, in celebration of the author's seventieth birthday.

It was an allegorical tale about a man who lives in a hut in the woods who attempts to tame a grey squirrel he finds with a broken leg. He nurses the animal back to health, feeds it and protects it, only for it to flee to freedom as soon as it is able. The man is upset, but eventually realises that he is like the squirrel, rejecting all those who have tried to help him.

Artemesia listened with mounting fury. It was *her* story. Four years earlier – she couldn't be sure of the date, but about then – she'd written something almost identical. It was a hedgehog, not a squirrel, that her man nursed back to health, and he realised it was his prickliness with people that isolated him, not his desire to be a free spirit, but the essence was the same. She switched off the radio, wandered around like a zombie from room to room, wondering what to do, and eventually made herself a strong pot of Earl Grey tea.

Two weeks later Artemesia was a delegate at the Short Story Writers' Association annual symposium, in Harrogate, and the anger had hardly subsided. Mixing and chatting with fellow authors, she'd decided, and casually relating the tale of the 'fantastically coincidental' similar story, was the ideal way to erode Jessica Fullerton's reputation.

'Of course,' she would tell anyone who was listening, 'I don't think for a second that anything untoward has taken place, and dear Jessica's story was much better than mine, but it does make one think, doesn't it?'

And think they did. There's no copyright on a good plot, but it was reprehensible for a writer to deliberately steal another's idea. Re-working an old story by someone long dead was acceptable – just – but when they were still alive and kicking… It wasn't done. It was after the Saturday evening dinner that Raoul Pawinski, resplendent in dinner suit with over-wide lapels, his moustache freshly razored to a thin line on his upper lip, approached Artemesia and, with the slightest trace of a bow, asked if he might have a word with her.

Pawinski was the son of a pilot who fought with the Free Polish Air Force in the Second World War. He was born in England, his mother a Land Army Girl who worked near the airfield where Pawinski Senior was stationed, but had inherited his father's clipped accent along with his Y chromosome. Actually, his normal speech marked him as a son of Lancashire, but he'd long ago found that a foreign accent was attractive to ladies, and gave him an opening to explain his exotic, much embellished, origins.

'Mrs Jones,' he said, 'I wonder if I could possibly tear you away from your friends and have a quiet word with you. Perhaps we could have coffee…?'

Artemesia, who had no friends, felt something inside her turn over. She'd been trying to decide whether to sit alone on one of the big easy chairs in the lounge, hoping that someone interesting would join her, or tag on to the usual group of misfits she always found herself with. Pawinski's approach changed all that. He was dashing and handsome, in a theatrical sort of way. She'd seen him at many similar functions but never spoken to him. It was common knowledge that he'd been married three times, and gossip said that he'd been a test pilot and one of the first men to break the sound barrier, but otherwise he was something of a mystery. He evidently earned a living from writing, but not in his real name. Once, in a story called *Clouds of Passion*, she'd modelled the hero on him.

'Why, Mr Pawinski,' Artemesia said, turning on a smile like one of the searchlights his father used to dodge, 'that would be delightful. Shall we repair to the lounge, where it's more comfortable?' Had his heels really clicked when he gave her that hint of a bow, she wondered?

Pawinski steered her on to one of the big leather settees and sat next to her, closer than she'd expected. He'd overdone the aftershave, she observed.

'First of all, Mrs Jones,' he said, 'I'd like to compliment you on that dress you are wearing. The colours are so subtle, and they go so well with your jewellery. Elegant and understated, just like the lady herself, eh?' He smiled and his pencil-line moustache curled up at the ends.

'Oh, please, call me Artemesia,' she gushed. 'You're so kind.' She fingered her necklace and wondered what had happened to the three Mrs Pawinskis.

'And you must call me Raoul,' he told her.

To rhyme with growl, she thought.

He ordered coffee and turned his attention back to Artemesia. 'I'm very interested in what you were saying, earlier, about Jessica Fullerton,' he confided. 'Something very similar happened to me.'

Artemesia swung her knees towards him and leaned forward. 'With Jessica?' she asked, unable to conceal her excitement.

'Yes, with Miss Fullerton.'

'Tell me about it. Please.'

'There's not much to tell. Two years ago I wrote a story about a paramedic who falls in love with an actress he helps after she crashes her sports car, and a year later I found something remarkably similar in one of the dear lady's collections. Mine was called "Love in the Fast Lane", hers "Hard Shoulder". Like you, I put it down to coincidence, but what you have said has made me wonder.'

'It's always been a mystery to me where she gets her ideas from,' Artemesia said. 'They're always so varied, and she comes up with them like... like...' a suitable simile failed to produce itself, but Pawinski came to the rescue:

'Stealing them would explain a lot,' he said.

'It would,' she agreed. 'Was your story published?'

'Regrettably, no.'

'But you submitted it?'

'Oh yes, it did the rounds.'

'Where exactly?'

Pawinski reeled off the names of all the major women's magazines and Artemesia was dismayed to hear that his target publications were much loftier than her modest ambitions. The fact that he'd been rejected by them all mollified the disappointment.

'Anywhere else?' she asked.

'None that I remember.'

'Positive?'

'Yes, I think so.'

The coffee arrived and Pawinski insisted on pouring it and adding her cream and sugar, which she would much have preferred to do herself. He did that ridiculous thing with a spoon and the cream, so it floated on the surface.

Artemesia was about to make her point by stirring in the cream and adding more sugar, although she didn't want more, when Pawinski said: 'There was one other place to which I submitted the manuscript.'

'Yes?' Artemesia encouraged, lowering the spoon.

'I entered it in the Allerton Bywater festival short story competition.'

She nearly knocked her cup over with excitement. 'The Allerton Bywater festival!' she echoed.

'Yes.'

'That's where I sent my story. That's how she's doing it. She knows the organiser and he's letting her look at all the entries. She steals the ideas. It's a big prize so must get hundreds – thousands – of entries. God, no wonder we all thought she had such a fertile imagination.'

'The rules state that your manuscript will not be returned,' Pawinski said. 'So when it's all over she simply collects all the non-winning entries and looks through them at her leisure. She takes the idea and writes it up in her own style, improving on the original. Not a difficult thing for someone like her.'

'Well I never! What are we going to do?'

'I don't know.'

'We can't let her get away with it.'

'That's true, but we have no proof.'

Some other people came to join them, curtailing the discussion, so they made vague noises about talking later and turned to welcome the newcomers.

They had an interesting conversation about agents and publishers, with Artemesia hanging on to every word that the others uttered. She'd never had two works published by the same people, so all the talk about editorial interference, royalties and deadlines was a mystery to her. She listened with a mixture of admiration and envy, pleased to be included in the conversation. At ten o'clock Pawinski excused himself and got drunk, leaning on the bar, and at ten thirty Artemesia left the group to go to bed. As she moved away from them two more delegates that she vaguely knew detached themselves from a knot of people standing near the bar and approached her.

'Artemesia,' the man said. 'Could we have a word, please?'

He was called Hillary Stubbs although he removed an l from his name for the medical romances that he wrote. Artemesia had always assumed that he was a retired doctor, but his only medical training was a certificate in first aid earned many years earlier when he worked for his local council. Two nervous breakdowns caused by the stress of examinations as a young man had destined him to a life of low-paid jobs. Writing had given him a new lease on life. For some, it really is cathartic.

'Why certainly,' Artemesia replied, gazing into his face. He was the cleanest, most well-scrubbed man she'd ever seen, and she wondered if he applied talcum powder to his cheeks.

'Do you know Sonia Cribbage?' he asked, indicating the small plump woman who had accompanied him as they'd pounced on Artemesia.

'Yes, of course,' she replied, extending a hand, although they had never actually spoken before now.

Half an hour later Artemesia resumed her journey up to bed, but her emotions were now a maelstrom of competing feelings. Indignation and anger whirled around inside her, jostling with moral outrage and a strange feeling of justification. She was going to enjoy destroying Jessica Fullerton, whatever way she chose to do it.

Both Hillary Stubbs and Sonia Cribbage had seen stories they'd written subsequently attributed to Miss Fullerton. One was published in an anthology, one broadcast by the BBC. Both stories had been entered for the Allerton Bywater festival short story competition. Artemesia took a sleeping pill before she laid her head on the pillow. An hour later she took another and eventually fell into a restless sleep.

The Sunday morning speaker was introduced as a publisher, although her actual position in the company was typing pool supervisor, who explained what her magazine was looking for. Then the organising chairman thanked everyone for their attendance, looked forward to seeing them next year and wished everyone who wasn't staying for lunch a safe journey home. Artemesia, Hillary, Sonia and Raoul met in the lounge, as they had arranged the night before, and ordered coffee.

Artemesia, after quickly and somewhat rudely grabbing the cream and fixing her own drink, explained why they were there. Jessica Fullerton must know someone involved with the Allerton Bywater festival short story competition, she told the others. That was the common denominator. They'd sent their best efforts to the competition, lured by the £500 first prize, and Jessica was given a free rein to look at, or possibly even take away, all the entries that didn't win prizes.

'She read our stories and used the ideas she liked most,' Artemesia concluded.

'And we paid £5 each for the privilege,' Pawinski said, remembering the entrance fee.

After a moment's silence, as the situation sank in, Sonia Cribbage said: 'The cow!'

'The bloody bitch!' Hillary Stubbs agreed.

'The fat bastard!' Raoul Pawinski added.

Artemesia was taken back by their vehemence, but felt justified by it. 'So what are we going to do?' she asked.

'Expose her,' someone suggested. 'Go to the press, show her up for what she is.'

'She'll deny it, say it's all coincidences.'

'And meanwhile the publicity will send her sales through the roof.'

'That's true.'

'So what's the alternative?'

They sat in silence for nearly a minute. Stubbs sipped his coffee, Pawinski stroked his chin. It was Sonia Cribbage who put the unthinkable into words.

'Kill her!' she said.

Three pairs of eyes turned to her.

'Yes, kill her. I slaved over that story, wrote it from the heart. I don't have a gift, like she has. I have to work at it, to struggle. I wanted to write since I was five years old, but I had to go to work for a living. I supported elderly parents and a dying husband. I wrote my first story in an exercise book while sitting at his bedside. People like Jessica Fullerton make me sick. They steal from other people just as surely as if they'd broken into our houses and robbed us, but without the risk. I hate her.'

Another silence, until Pawinski said: 'I agree. Kill her.'

Artemesia looked at Hillary Stubbs. He caught her gaze and gave a slow nod of agreement.

'So,' she said, 'that's settled, then. The only question now is: How?'

'For goodness sake,' Sonia replied, irritated. 'We're writers, aren't we? If we can't think of a way, who can?'

Pawinski, true to his East European origins, said: 'A bomb. Blow her up. Boom! No evidence.'

'I'm for shooting her,' Hillary Stubbs told them. 'A bullet in the head. It's clean and it's merciful.'

Artemesia turned to the other woman. 'A blunt instrument has always been my favourite MO,' Sonia Cribbage confessed. 'One is always readily available, and if applied with sufficient conviction it's as deadly as a bullet.'

'Thank you, Sonia,' Artemesia said. 'That leaves me. I'm a poisoner. Poison has a certain subtlety that has always appealed to me.'

❖

Hillary Stubbs glanced nervously over his shoulder and crossed the road. He was in an area of the city where he'd never ventured before. If you believed the local newspaper, drug dealing and prostitution were the norm around here, and Stubbs, like most white people, believed it. What he saw did nothing to persuade him otherwise. All the shops had metal grills over the windows and litter blew in eddies on every corner. Two youths in woolly hats standing outside the Hakuna Matata electrical emporium watched him as he stepped onto the pavement and Stubbs was glad that he had no money on his person.

Before they left the conference the Famous Four had agreed that each would pursue their chosen method of execution to evaluate the practicalities. They would then meet, two weeks later, to finalise a plan. Hillary Stubbs' task was to procure a firearm.

Either of the two youths in woolly hats would have done, but Stubbs was nervous at the thought of being outnumbered. Several other people walked by but each time he thought of an excuse not to talk to them. As he walked back down the street, in front of a parade of shops, a tall man in a sparkling white T-shirt and dreadlocks came out of the newsagents, perusing a folded paper. It was now or never.

'Um, excuse me,' Stubbs said.

The man blinked big brown eyes and looked at him.

'I wonder if you can help me?'

'I'll try,' the man replied, tucking the paper under his arm.

'Right. Well, er, thank you. The truth is, I'm trying to purchase a gun.'

'A gun?'

'Um, yes. Not a big gun, just, you know, a pistol. Not a real one. A replica. A real one would do, of course. Might even be better. Replicas never look quite right, don't you think?'

The man looked puzzled and bemused. 'What do you want a gun for?'

'Oh, it's er, it's er, for a play I'm producing. Um, *Annie Get Your Gun*. Not a play, a musical. Couldn't have a title like that without a gun in it, could you?'

'No, I don't suppose you could. Have you tried a theatrical suppliers?'

'Theatrical suppliers? No, I haven't. Do you think they might have one?'

'Bound to have. There's one on Regent Street, near the clock.'

'Right. Thanks for your help. I'm very grateful.'

'No problem,' the man said, and strode away shaking his head.

Stubbs stood awhile before walking off in the opposite direction, bathed in sweat and trembling with embarrassment. The man was probably a doctor or a lawyer, he told himself. He had an educated accent.

The two youths in the woolly hats were still outside the electrical store, sitting on the rail put there to discourage ram raids. They wore jogging bottoms six sizes too large, hooded tops and big trainers with the laces undone. Stubbs, feeling strangely emboldened by the earlier encounter, approached them.

'Hey boys, I need some help,' he said.

'Help? Waddya want, man?' one of them replied.

'I need a little favour doing. For which I'll pay, of course.'

'Hey, man, we're big on favours, ain't we, Lloyd?'

'Sure is, man. Favours is our strongpoint. Just afore I came out mah mamma sez to me: "You ged oud dere and do some favours, boy, or you ain't no son o' mine."'

Stubbs smiled with satisfaction. This was more like it. 'Fact is, boys, I need a shooter,' he confided.

'A shoodah?'

'Yeah, a shooter.'

'What's a shoodah?'

'You know.' He demonstrated with an outstretched forefinger.

'You mean a gun?'

'Yeah, a gun. A revolver.'

'Wow, man. That's wicked. You're talking big Gs there, mistah.'

'Can you help me?'

'Ah do' know. Waddya think, Lloyd?'

'Hey, man. This is bad stuff. We don't normally do heavy stuff like dat.'

'Do you know anyone who might help me?'

'Hey, waid a minute, man. Ah didn't say we couldn't help you, just that, ya know, we haven't seen your credentials, like.' He rubbed a thumb and forefinger together to show exactly what credentials he meant.

'Oh, I can pay,' Stubbs assured them. 'I haven't any money on me but I can get some. How much will we be talking about?'

'Dunno. Need to talk to someone.'

'I'd be grateful if you would.'

The boy pulled a state-of-the-art Sony cell phone from a pocket, flipped it open and walked away, out of earshot. Stubbs tried having a conversation with the remaining youth but abandoned it after a few barely intelligible replies.

Lloyd came back, still holding the phone to his ear. 'Yoose in luck, man,' he told Stubbs. 'Mah contact has just taken delivery of a nice liddle shoodah that he's willing to pass on to you as a special favour.'

'How much?' Stubbs asked.

'Two hundred big ones.'

Stubbs had read a newspaper article that said guns could be obtained for as little as £100. 'One hundred,' he said.

Lloyd relayed the message. 'One fifty,' he came back with.

'OK,' Stubbs told him. 'One fifty. It's a deal.'

'Great. Pleasure to do business wid you, man.' He held out a hand, palm up, and Stubbs slapped it like he'd seen on TV.

'You need bullets?' he was asked.

'Of course I need bullets.'

'Bullets is fifty.'

Stubbs agreed to be back in thirty minutes with the money. He went to a bank and drew £200 from the ATM with the debit card he'd concealed in his shoe. He slipped £100 in his trouser back pocket and £100 in his shirt pocket, in case of muggers. He was enjoying this, thinking like they thought, and he felt more alive than he'd done in his entire life. Streetwise, that's what it was called, and the material he was gathering that would be of use in stories was beyond belief. He slipped the card back into his shoe and strode off towards the assignation.

Raoul Pawinski's task was to make a bomb. As a schoolboy he'd learned that the magic ingredients were saltpetre, sulphur and carbon. As an adult he knew that fertilizer was used extensively in the manufacture of homemade explosives. He wasn't sure but he imagined that saltpetre was some sort of nitrate, as used in fertilizer. Charcoal would do for carbon, which just left the sulphur. He consulted Yellow Pages.

There were not many entries under Chemicals, but enough for his purpose. The first one he rang only dealt in chemicals for water treatment plants and the next one supplied the manufacturers of dyes. Yes, they did supply sulphur and would he like to open an account with them? He didn't.

After another couple of fruitless calls he decided that this was a futile avenue to follow. He went to the library and logged one of their computers on to the internet. 'How to make a bomb' produced immediate results. Pawinski pulled out a notebook and started writing furiously.

Batteries, he learned, were a source of magnesium oxide, which, when mixed with hydrogen peroxide, made a respectable explosion. He carefully copied the instructions right to the end, then lowered his pen in dismay. 'Shake well,' it said, 'then run away as fast as possible.'

That was no good. The idea was to leave the device under her car, primed to explode as soon as she drove off and completed the simple electrical circuit he'd already designed. He clicked the next entry.

There were bombs made from match heads, bombs made from fireworks, even detailed, step-by-step instructions on how to make an atom bomb, but he decided that one of those was over the top. Killing Jessica Fullerton was one thing, but wiping out half of the north of England in the pursuit of her demise would be counter-productive. Almost all of the entries had come from foul-mouthed, illiterate weirdos, probably in America. Those that weren't of the throw-and-run type required some sort of detonator to trigger the explosion, but the instructions for obtaining detonators never went beyond 'steal them'. Pawinski closed his notebook and wondered if the whole thing had been such a good idea.

Sonia Cribbage eyed the blue and steel wrecking bar in the window of the Ace DIY store and decided it was just what she wanted. And it wasn't expensive, either.

'Ah, you mean a jemmy,' the thin man behind the counter replied when she asked for one. 'We sell a lot of these. Not taking up burglary, I hope, Madam.'

'No,' Sonia replied with a smile, deciding not to add 'Murder' by way of explanation. 'It's for raising some crazy paving.'

'Heavy work,' he told her as he placed the bar in a bag. 'Don't attempt it yourself.'

She thanked him and left the shop, surprised at how heavy the bag felt. One decent blow with that should finish off the most thick-skulled victim. Driving home she reconsidered that thought. One blow to incapacitate her; a second, really violent blow to finish her off and a third as insurance. That was how to do it, but first of all she'd experiment with the two over-ripe watermelons she'd purchased in the market.

Back in her own kitchen she pushed the table against the wall and moved the chairs out of the way. When there was sufficient room – to swing a jemmy, not a cat, she told herself with a grim smile – Sonia fetched a travelling rug from the bedroom cupboard and laid it in a crumpled heap on the floor. She placed the riper of the two melons on it and arranged the rug to hold it loosely in position.

Sonia picked up the jemmy and gave a few trial swings with it. If she held on to the bent end, she decided, there was less chance of it slipping from her grasp. She tapped the melon lightly, like a golfer taking a practice putt, then raised the jemmy above her head and brought it down with all her strength.

Thwack! She closed her eyes at the moment of impact and raised the jemmy again. *Spladge!* And again. *Splodge!*

Sonia opened her eyes to survey the damaged, noticing that she was puffing as much as when she climbed the stairs at the shopping mall. The melon had been reduced to a mass of pulp. Juice and seeds covered the kitchen floor and she realised that what she'd thought was perspiration running down her cheeks was more juice. The front of her dress was soaked in it. She raised her eyes to survey the walls and the ceiling and saw that they too were covered in the remnants of the melon. She tried to imagine what the real thing would look like, if the juice were arterial blood and the pips fragments of skull or brain, and felt herself swoon.

They met at the Mad Hatter teashop in Masham, north of Ripon, which was as central a location as they could find. Pawinski arrived deliberately early and lunched on steak and kidney pie followed by spotted dick. It was a small, if expensive, treat that he'd promised himself. He was wearing a belted tweed jacket with a high collar, even though it was a warm day, and cavalry twills. His size six shoes had brass strips around the toes and gleamed like moonlight on still water.

Hillary Stubbs was next to arrive. He wore pale blue lightweight slacks bought by mail order via the *Sunday Times* colour supplement and a Greenwoods zipper jacket in sage green. The women arrived together five minutes later, Artemesia in her customary flowered dress and Sonia looking cool in a crisp white blouse and pleated skirt. They shook hands with the men and exchanged air-kisses.

After tea and sandwiches, with Pawinski excusing himself from anything to eat on the grounds of mysterious dietary requirements, and the usual grumbles about the prices, they got down to business. Artemesia acted as chair person.

'I'm afraid I failed, miserably,' she confessed. 'My task was to come up with a way of poisoning Jessica, but it was harder than I expected. The poison bit was no problem, but I had to have a way of delivering it, and that's where I came undone. I rang her publisher, saying I wanted to invite her to a function, and they told me that she was in this country, not the Isle of Man, for the summer. She still owns a cottage in Robin Hood's Bay and the address is in the Association members' directory, so I went there.'

'You went there!' someone exclaimed.

'Yes. It's not too far for me. And if I was serious about this it was obvious we'd have to meet, somewhere along the line.'

'That's true,' Pawinski agreed, nodding with understanding.

'So what did you do?' Sonia asked.

'I followed her. I waited on a bench opposite her cottage. Incidentally, it's not as grand as I expected. Just a little thing in a terrace. Very neat, but quite small.'

'And probably worth about half a million,' Stubbs told them.

'Yes, I imagine so,' Artemesia replied. 'So,' she continued, 'after about three quarters of an hour Jessica came out and I followed her. She has a routine, which includes going for morning coffee to a certain café on the seafront at ten thirty every day. I'd had the foresight to arm myself with one of her books – *Lust in the Sun* – which is as dire a tome as you could imagine, and I seated myself facing her usual place. As my Earl Grey arrived I plucked up courage and approached her, asking if she was Jessica Fullerton, saying I was a great fan of hers, and could she possibly autograph my latest purchase. I apologised for interrupting her break and much to my surprise she invited me to join her.'

'She invited you to join her!' Sonia echoed.

'Yes, so I did. I had a scone and butter and she had a Welsh rarebit. It looked delicious. She doesn't do lunch, she said, but has a morning break and afternoon tea instead.'

'That's interesting,' Hillary Stubbs commented. 'Stopping for lunch does tend to disrupt the day when you're writing.'

'Oh, I couldn't do without a break to listen to *World at One*,' Sonia said.

'Never mind that,' Pawinski interrupted. 'What happened next?'

'Well, I casually mentioned that I did some writing and had had a modicum of success, and she was most interested. Well, actually, she sounded thrilled to bits. She invited me to have afternoon tea with her. Said she was having difficulty with a new story, about an unmarried mother. She said the boundaries were being pushed back a little further every year, but she didn't know how far she dare go with it. My opinion would be gratefully appreciated. Can you believe that? Jessica Fullerton asking for my opinion.'

Pawinski said: 'It sounds as if you would have plenty of opportunity to administer the fatal dose,' and all eyes turned back to Artemesia.

'Y-yes,' she stammered, 'b-but the truth is... I don't think I could do it. I-I rather liked her.'

There was a long, stunned silence. A waitress came and started clearing the table next to theirs. She squirted the surface with something from a spray and wiped it clean. After she'd left Pawinski said: 'So, it's all off, is it? It was your idea, you know. You started all this.'

'I know, and I've been thinking about it. What she did was still despicable, and we should go ahead, as planned, but I don't think I could do it. I just don't have the strength, or determination, or whatever it takes. What about the rest of you? What did you all come up with?'

Pawinski cleared his throat and looked at the ketchup bottle, Sonia fidgeted with her handbag and Stubbs drummed his fingers on the Formica and inspected the legs of the retreating waitress.

'Raoul?' Artemesia invited, wondering how many minutes he spent each morning perfecting his moustache. 'Did you have any luck?'

He shuffled in his chair and pulled himself up to his full height. 'No,' he confessed. 'I met certain difficulties. The current political climate makes it almost impossible to obtain the necessary precursors to manufacture a bomb. The security forces have techniques for listening to telephone traffic and picking out certain code words. Unfortunately I'm out of touch with all these new developments; things have changed since my day, and I may have inadvertently aroused their suspicions. I rang a few people – contacts from the old days – but they couldn't help me. I'm fairly certain my phone is now being tapped, so I had to back off.' He sagged into his chair again, happy to have impressed them, even if he had failed with his mission.

'Oh dear,' Artemesia said. 'Do you think you will be all right?'

'Ah! No problem.' He dismissed her concern with a wave of his hand. 'What the heck,' he said. 'They can only stick burning matches down my fingernails.'

She turned to Stubbs. 'And what about you, Hillary? You were trying to obtain a gun, I believe.'

'Ye-es.' He was wearing a cravat under the collar of his checked shirt, and suddenly seemed to be finding it a little tight. He eased it with his fingers. 'I'm afraid I came up with the same problem as Raoul. Things are tight, out there on the street. I spoke to some people but guns aren't as easy to come by as you might imagine. I was promised one, at a fair price, but was let down at the last moment. By then, I too was probably arousing suspicion, so I had to abandon the attempt.' The attempt had cost him £200. Had he produced a gun he'd have been happy to ask them to share the cost, but they wouldn't give him £50 each for nothing, to pay for his stupidity. He'd given Lloyd the £200 and he'd gone off to fetch the weapon, with the other boy staying behind as security. After half an hour the youth suggested he go see what had happened to Lloyd, and Stubbs had no option other than to agree. That was the last he saw of either of them and the money. An hour later he went home, poorer and wiser, but he didn't relate this part of the story to the other three.

Raoul nodded his understanding and Artemesia thanked him for trying. She turned to Sonia Cribbage. 'That just leaves you, Sonia,' she said.

Sonia took three deep breaths and launched herself into a blow-by-blow account – literally – of the great watermelon massacre that had taken place in her kitchen. It had taken her three days to clean up the mess and her home still smelled of over-ripe fruit juice. She asked them to imagine what it would be like if the stains on the walls, ceiling, floor and her clothing had been skin and bone, blood and tissue, brains and eyeballs and everything else that goes into the making of a human head. She shuddered at the thought and told them that no way could she countenance this way of ridding themselves of the plagiarising Jessica Fullerton.

Secretly, they were all slightly relieved by the outcome, but none of them would admit it. Stubbs lifted the teapot, testing it, but it was empty. Pawinski wondered if the ring on Sonia Cribbage's third finger, right hand, was a real diamond. He reckoned it was, and estimated it at about two carats. Sonia leaned slightly away from him, repulsed by his aftershave. The expression 'snake oil' sprang into her mind and she smiled inwardly.

'So that's it. We've failed,' Artemesia told them, and they all nodded.

'Perhaps it's for the best,' she added after a suitable silence. 'I don't think we're cut out to be murderers.' More nods of agreement.

'And it's been a learning experience for all of us,' Sonia declared. This time Hillary Stubbs didn't join in the nodding. The learning experience had cost him £200. He knew where he could have done a lot more learning for £200.

'So what are we going to do, let her get away with it?' Pawinski demanded. 'Let's not forget that she stole our stories.'

'And probably lots of other people's,' Stubbs said. 'We're probably just the tip of the iceberg.'

'I've been thinking about that,' Sonia told them, and all eyes turned to her. 'We could do what we do best,' she explained.

'Murder,' Pawinski interjected. 'We do murder best, and we've failed.'

'No we don't. We're writers, not murderers. We should write about her.'

'Write about her?' the others repeated in unison.

'Yes, write about her. A short story exposing her.'

'We'd never get it published.'

'That doesn't matter. We could try, but if nobody will touch it we just send it to her. Let her know that her little game is up.'

'*Mein Gott!*' Pawinski exclaimed. 'It could be the answer.'

'The pen is mightier than the sword,' said Artemesia.

'Let's have some more tea and work through it,' Stubbs suggested.

He and Artemesia went to fetch the tea and while they were gone Pawinski told Sonia that her hair looked particularly nice today. She thanked him and placed her handbag on the floor between them.

Stubbs returned, carrying a heavily laden tray and acted as mother, a role he fell into as easily as a student falls into bed. 'Now,' he said, his domestic duties concluded, 'How do we handle this?' Like the others, he was greatly relieved that murder was no longer on the agenda.

Sonia cleared her throat and looked up from the shorthand pad on which she'd been making notes. 'Well,' she began, 'I'd be happy to have a go at the story. Perhaps you could help me, Artemesia, as we don't live too far apart?'

Artemesia nodded her agreement with enthusiasm. Sonia Cribbage was much more successful than she was, and working with her might be an education. Suddenly, the whole project was looking worthwhile, not the dangerous adventure it had nearly become.

'How long do you need?' Stubbs asked. 'We could all meet here again when you have a first draft ready.'

Sonia looked at Artemesia, who was about to suggest a month when Sonia said: 'Two weeks should be ample, don't you think, Artemesia?'

'Oh, er, yes, that should be more than ample,' she replied.

'That's agreed then. We meet here two weeks today. Is that convenient for you, Raoul?'

Pawinski shuffled in his seat, gave a terse little nod in answer to the question, then asked: 'And what are we going to call this story? And whom are we going to say it is by? Don't forget we

have libel laws in this country and Ms Fullerton could probably afford to ruin us all.'

'That's a good point,' Stubbs agreed. 'In cases like this, having a
big bank account is more useful than having right on your side.'

'Oh dear, I don't want to become involved in litigation,'
Artemesia said. 'I had enough of that when… when… well,
I just don't.'

'It won't come to litigation,' Stubbs assured her. 'We'll just
have to be careful to keep our identities concealed.'

'But we want to be able to demonstrate that it was us who
wrote the story,' Sonia declared. 'Some time in the future we
might want to say it was us who wrote it.'

They nodded their agreements. It would be a shame to
write such a good story anonymously. One day they might
want to claim the credit for it.

'I know!' Pawinski declared, banging his fist on the table and
causing Sonia to spill her tea. 'An anagram. Have the story be
by someone whose name is an anagram of ours.' He sat back
with the satisfaction of a man who had just solved the riddle
of dark matter.

'It would have to be a long name,' Stubbs commented.
Finding an anagram that would have to include Polish names
amongst the possibilities did not sound like a fruitful exercise.
Pawinski threw him a glare.

Sonia dabbed her notebook dry with a paper serviette. 'It
doesn't have to be an anagram,' she said. 'Look. I've written our
names down.' She turned the notebook so the others could
read it. 'I'm sure we could make something out of them.'

Hillary Stubbs reached for the book and studied the list.
'Ye-es,' he agreed, adding: 'Look, if I go over one syllable in
each of our names, like this…' He took the list and worked
on it for a few seconds, '…to make those letters bolder, and
perhaps underline them for a bit more emphasis, so they look
like this…' He pushed the notebook back across the table for
the others to consider.

The list now read:

Hillary **Stu**bbs
Artemesia Jones
Raoul **Paw**inski
Sonia Cribbage

'It's not much of a name,' Sonia said.

'It doesn't roll off the tongue,' Artemesia agreed. 'And it's not very memorable.'

'No,' Stubbs concurred, 'but it fulfils our purpose.'

Pawinski flapped a hand in approval, saying: 'Its forgettable-ness is what makes it so suitable, and it would be impossible to link it to the four of us, which is the main intention,' and the two ladies nodded.

'Which just leaves a title,' Stubbs said.

Pawinski smiled and held his cupped hand out in front of him, like a great orator about to deliver the goods. 'In Poland,' he told them, 'there is a saying: "Revenge is a dish that is…"'

'Yes,' Sonia Cribbage interrupted with a laugh. 'We have the same saying here, Raoul. But I think you've given us our title.'

Stubbs smiled in agreement and Artemesia sat back as a warm feeling of satisfaction engulfed her. She was among like minds, she thought. She belonged. And that was more important than anything else. She looked at her three new friends and three new stories popped into her head.

'More tea, anybody?' she asked.

Ann Cleeves

Basic Skills

Maddy thought books could change lives. That was what she'd told Sylvia at the interview for the post of literacy tutor. Sylvia, who was in charge of access at MMU, had given a cynical little smile, but had given Maddy the job anyway. Perhaps there wasn't much competition. Certainly the pay was dreadful. The project was an attempt to encourage local people to consider further education, to give them, Sylvia said, a fresh start. It was a fresh start for Maddy too. A return to confidence after the end of a long-term relationship. A change of career.

Now, walking through Didsbury Park to her first class, Maddy felt the same excitement as she had as a child at the beginning of the school year. She loved the romance of autumn. The leaves were starting to turn and there was a freshness in the air after a long, humid summer. In her bag she carried a new pencil case and a file with all her students' names. At the university she waited for her students in a room which smelled of worn gym kit and floor polish. In the street below, the lights came on.

The students drifted in one at a time. She greeted them all, holding out her hand, repeating their names. Knew she was being too effusive as soon as she opened her mouth, felt the smile too wide, her voice a little too loud. She should have worn jeans. Her clothes were showy and seemed designed to set her apart. She wanted to tell her students that she'd got the garments at cost, that she'd been in the business once. Instead she grinned and made more unnecessary introductions.

They sat at their little tables and stared at her. She marked them off the register, trying to memorise their names. Sophie was the thin one with the staring eyes. Alan had the nervous laugh. There were seven of them. One was missing – an eighteen-year-old called Anthony who lived in a probation hostel. Sylvia had said he might not turn up.

They're unpredictable, the hostel lads. We can't force them after all.

During her training Maddy had observed other literacy classes and thought how tedious they were. How patronising. She was passionate about reading. How could her students not respond?

She was just starting on her prepared introduction when the missing student walked in. He had soft hair and sad brown eyes. His face was framed by the hood of his parka. He had an edgy tension which made her think he might be an addict.

'Sorry I'm late, miss.' As if he was still at school. He had a lovely smile.

She started them reading first lines. Interesting first lines from her favourite writers. Margaret Atwood. Charlotte Brontë. Carol Shields. She'd printed the words very big on thick, white paper. Then she asked what might come next in the book.

'Don't you want to find out?' she demanded. 'Really, can you bear not to know?'

The students smiled indulgently at her and looked at the clock. They'd been told there'd be a break halfway through the session. Free tea and biscuits.

They came back late, licking chocolaty fingers and smelling of cigarettes.

'If you were to write your own story, where would you start?' Maddy asked. 'Give me a first line! Don't worry about the spelling, just get the words down.'

She wasn't sure if Anthony had heard her. He stared in front of him, features rigid. Then he leaned very close to his paper and started to write. The point of his tongue was clamped between his lips in concentration.

'Who shall we start with?' Maddy asked brightly. 'Anthony, what about you?' Already she was fascinated by him.

He looked up at her and she thought he might refuse to read his work. She decided she wouldn't make a big deal of it.

Then he spoke.

'*The buckle shaped like a ship on the belt my father beat me with,*' he said. 'That's what I'd start with.'

He spoke slowly, rhythmically. Like a poet, making every word count. She was moved almost to tears.

'Anthony, that's a stunning piece of writing.'

He became her star student. He brought her scraps of verse and ideas for stories. Most of his writing was sentimental and childish, but there were pieces so powerful that they took her breath away.

On the third week he asked about her favourite book.

'*The Catcher in the Rye,*' she said immediately. 'You should try it. Really, it's only short. You could manage it. Come back with me now and you can borrow it.' She was swept away by the idea that he would love the book too.

He waited while she packed away her papers and tucked her glasses in their case and they walked slowly through the fallen leaves.

'What's it like in the hostel?' she asked.

'Not so bad.' He was standing under a light and she caught a quick, bleak smile. 'I'm hoping to get a place of my own soon.'

She didn't ask why he was living there. She felt it would be bad manners to pry.

In the flat, she poured him a glass of Rioja, because that was what she would have done with any of her friends. He sat opposite her, sipping the wine as if it was medicine. He told her his father was dead now. 'Cancer, poor bastard, but he went out fighting as always.' Then he left, with the book in his pocket. From her window on the first floor, she watched him go. He stopped once to look back.

Her friends were horrified by her folly in letting him know where she lived.

'Are you crazy? You don't even know why he's caught up with the probation service. He could be violent.'

'Oh, I don't think so.'

It was early October, a bright clear day. They were sitting outside Tilly's Café & Bar in Chorlton, drinking cappuccino.

A Saturday morning ritual. She looked at their shocked faces and saw that perhaps she had been foolish. How could she have been so naïve?

She began to distance herself from Anthony. In class she picked skeletal Sophie or serious Maz to read first. She looked at Anthony's poems and stories when everyone else was there, read into them a suppressed violence which she hadn't previously noticed. What previously she had considered powerful, now she read as disturbed. After class, she rushed off immediately, claiming meetings, dinner with a boyfriend who didn't exist. Anthony sat at the front and looked at her.

One evening in her flat, after she'd eaten, she poured herself a second glass of wine and stood with it looking into the street. There was a fine drizzle which looked like mist. Halfway along the road, leaning against a tree, was a dark figure with a hood pulled over his head. Anthony. She let the curtain fall, felt her pulse quicken, saw that the surface of the wine was trembling, realised her hand must be shaking. When she found the courage to look out again, he'd gone.

The next day she had the locks on her flat changed. She'd lost her spare key some time ago and hadn't thought much of it. She had never been very tidy – one of the sources of discontent with Des. Now she tried to remember if she'd seen it since Anthony's visit. It tormented her that a kind and spontaneous invitation could lead to this unease. She knew it was her fault but she blamed Anthony. Whenever she thought of him now she was taken over by a sense of dread. In class she could hardly look at him.

The certainty that she was being followed developed over several days. There was nothing she could pin down. Nothing rational. A figure disappearing into thick fog when she left home early one morning to buy milk. A shadow thrown across the pavement when she walked back from college. Once she definitely saw him, huddled against a cold east wind, hands in pockets, head bent. He was walking along the street behind her. She sensed him or heard his footsteps, turned suddenly and caught his eye. He looked defiant but rather pitiful. She hurried on, could hear him behind her, running, but not quite catching her before she turned into her flat.

Before she closed the door he shouted after her. She couldn't make out the words; the wind seemed to snatch them away and she pictured them rolling down the street like dead leaves. Inside, standing with her back to the door, she felt sick and panicky. The last time she'd felt like this was when Des had told her their relationship was over. He'd fallen for a colleague. They'd decided to settle down and have kids. She'd vowed never to let a man get to her like that again, but here she was, in her own flat, wanting to throw up all over the carpet.

She stood there for a long time. The phone rang. It couldn't be Anthony. She was ex-directory and had never been silly enough to give him her number. She waited for a message to be left on the answering machine but the caller hung up. At last she moved, walked through to the kitchen, looked out of the window. The street was empty. She lifted the phone to ring her friends, but replaced it. She couldn't bear their *I told you so* sympathy. They'd thought all the time that she was stupid, that she'd be lost without Des, that it was ridiculous to teach losers to read.

Later she felt an emptiness which could have been hunger and she hacked herself a slice from a crusty loaf. The knife was short and squat, very sharp. After the bread was cut, she wiped crumbs from the knife's blade and put it into her handbag. That evening, as she stared mindlessly at a television drama, her thoughts returned occasionally to its steely sharpness, bringing her comfort, the nearest she'd been to calm for days.

It was the last class before the October half term and the students were in a cheerful mood. Maddy realised that they'd become friends. Sophie had lost her haunted look and was chatting about the care home where she worked. Anthony hadn't arrived and Maddy started the class without him. Perhaps she was free of him, he'd drifted off or been arrested again. But he walked in late as he had for the first session, with the same edginess and pleading eyes. She forced herself to be polite, took courage from thought of the knife, sharpened that morning, which lay in the bottom of her handbag.

Towards the end of the lesson though, her nerve failed her and she finished the class early. Her students gathered around her desk.

'We're going to the pub, Maddy. Will you come too?'

'Sorry,' she said. 'I'm not feeling too brilliant actually. I think I'll go straight home.' There was no point now, conjuring up the imaginary boyfriend. Anthony had been following her and knew he didn't exist.

She was going by the side of the park when she heard the footsteps following, light and quick. She walked more firmly, with her right hand she opened the bag which was slung over her shoulder, gripped the steel handle.

His touch shocked her. He'd never touched her before, not even to shake her hand. This was tentative, a stroke on her shoulder. Maddy felt her throat constrict as if she was already being strangled, turned and struck, with the knife in her clenched fist.

There was a gasp, a whisper and Sophie fell. Lying on the pavement she seemed even smaller and more delicate than she had in class. Her skirt had ridden above her knees and her legs were thin and white. In one hand she still held the purse Maddy had left on her desk before hurrying out of class.

Cath Staincliffe

Laptop

I'd been boosting laptops for a couple of years but never with such bloody disastrous consequences. Up until then it'd been easy money. Two or three a week kept body and soul together and was a damn sight more conducive to the good life than temping in some god-awful office with all the crap about diets and botox and endless squabbles over the state of the kitchen. Shorter working week, too. Eight, maybe ten hours, the rest of the time my own.

I always dressed well for work – part of the scam, isn't it? People are much less guarded if I'm in a designer suit: something smart, fully lined, along with good shoes, hair and make-up. Helps me mingle. Looking like an executive, some high-flying businesswoman, gives me access to the most fertile picking grounds: conference centres, business parks, commuter trains, the best restaurants and coffee bars. And, after all, if someone nicks your laptop who's going to spring to mind? Me with my crisp clothes, my detached air, snag-free tights or some lad in a beanie hat and dirty fingernails?

So, that fateful day, as I came to think of it, I was working at Manchester Airport. I do it four or five times a year; the train service is handy and with all the business flights I've plenty of targets to choose from.

As with any type of thieving, opportunity is all. The aim being to get the goods and get away with it. When I started working for Danny, he came out with me, but I was quick on the uptake and after a few runs he left me to it. I'm one of his best operators but he reckons I'm lazy. You could make more, he tells me near enough every time I swap the merchandise for cash, a bit of ambition you could be clearing fifty a year, higher tax bracket. The last bit's a joke. No one in the business pays any tax. But I'm not greedy. I enjoy the time I have. Gives me chance to indulge my passion. I paint watercolours. Surprised? So was I when I first drifted into it. Then it became the centre of my life. It was what got me out of bed and kept me up late.

That day when I spotted the mark I dubbed him The Wolf. He had a large head, the coarse brown hair brushed straight back from his face, a long, sharp nose and lips that didn't quite meet; too many teeth for his mouth. Like a kid with those vampire fangs stuffed in their gob. I assumed he was meeting someone as he made no move to check in and we were near the arrivals hall. He had the laptop on the floor, to his right, at the side of his feet. He was in prime position at the end of a row of seats, in the lounge where people have coffee while they wait for the information boards to change or for a disembodied voice to make hard-to-hear announcements.

After walking about a bit, checking my exit routes and getting a feel for the atmosphere that day and the people hanging around (no nutters, drunks or a surfeit of security guards) I settled myself on the end seat of the row adjoining his. He and I were back to back. I put my large bag down beside me at my left. My bag and his laptop were maybe five inches apart. On the seat next to me I put my own laptop and handbag. When I turned to my left I could see us both reflected in the plain glass of the offices that ran along the edge of the concourse. There were coloured screens behind the glass to mask the work areas so no danger of my being seen from in there.

Timing is crucial. I watched his reflection as he glanced down to check his laptop and I moved a few seconds after, just as a large family with raucous kids and two trolley-loads of bags hoved into view, squabbling about where to wait. Keeping my upper body straight, I reached my left arm back and grasped the handle of his laptop, pulled it forward and lifted it up and into my big bag. I grabbed the handles of that, hitched it onto my shoulder, collected my other things, stood and walked steadily away. Belly clamped, mouth dry, senses singing.

Twice I've been rumbled at that very moment, before I'm out of range. Both in the early days. Turning, I look confused. 'Sorry?'

'My laptop!' They are incandescent with outrage, ready to thump me. Except I don't run or resist. I gawp at them, look completely befuddled, furrowed brow. Mouth the word 'laptop?' My hand flies to my mouth, I stare in my bag. 'Oh, my god.' Both hands to my mouth. I blush furiously. Wrestle the shopper from my shoulder. 'God, I am so sorry.' Withdraw the offending article, hand it back, talking all the time, on the brink of tears. 'It's exactly like mine.' I hold up my own laptop (case only: I'm not lugging around something that heavy all day – besides someone might nick it). 'I was miles away, oh, god, I feel awful. You must think, oh, please I am so, so sorry. I don't know what to say.' Deliberately making a scene, drawing attention, flustered woman in a state. Their expressions morph: rage, distrust, exasperation, embarrassment and eventually relief tinged with discomfort. They just want me to shut up and disappear. Which I do.

With The Wolf, though, all goes smooth as silk.
Until I get the bastard thing home and open it.

I generally check to see if they're password protected. Danny has a little code that cracks about fifty per cent of them, the rest he passes on to a geek who sorts them out. Danny appreciates it if I let him know which ones need further attention when I hand them over.

So I got home, changed into something more comfortable, had lunch on my little balcony. On a clear day to the east I can see the hills beyond the City of Manchester stadium and the velodrome and to the west the city centre: a jumble of Victorian gothic punctuated by modern glass and steel, wood and funny angles, strong colours. It's a vista I love to paint. But that day was damp, hazy, shrouding the skyline. I polished off a smoked salmon salad, some green tea, then got down to business.

Danny's code didn't work. And I could have left it at that. I should have. But there was a memory stick there: small, black, inoffensive looking. I picked it up and slotted it into the USB port on my own machine. There wasn't much on it, that's what I thought at the time, just one file, called *Accounts*. I opened it expecting credits and debits, loss carried forward or whatever. Perhaps bank details that Danny could milk. Overseas accounts, savings.

Not those sort of accounts.

June 12th 2010
She was very drunk when she left the club. Falling into a taxi, falling out at her place. I let her get inside and waited for a while before I went in the back. She was stumbling about for long enough. When I judged she was asleep I crept upstairs. I had everything ready. She woke. But I'd done it by then. The colour flooded her face and she tried to get up, jerking, but couldn't, then the flush drained away and her eyes glazed over. I closed her eyes. She looked more peaceful that way. It was wonderful. Better than I'd imagined. A pure rush. Cleaner, brighter than drugs or religion or sex. On a different plane. I wish I'd stayed there longer now. I didn't want to leave her but I was being cautious. Everything meticulously done. Precise, tidy. I've waited all my life for this. I wasn't going to ruin it by being clumsy and leaving anything they could trace back to me.

June 18th 2010
Lady Luck must be smiling down on me. No one suspects a thing.

The Wolf obviously fancied himself as a scribe. Some sort of crime thriller. I wondered if he'd got this backed up anywhere else or if he'd just lost his life's work. I read on. I mainly read biographies but it was intriguing. The next entry was a couple of months later.

Aug 23rd 2010
I'm getting restless again. Low after the high? Things are difficult. I can't remember her face anymore. I should have taken a photograph.

Sept 4th 2010
I've found the next one. Not sure how to get in but the good weather might make things easier. An open window, patio doors? She has a beautiful face; very simple, strong mouth, wide eyes. I want to see those eyes change.

A tinge of unease made me pause. I scrolled down the document – it was only four pages long. I scanned it all again. The dates spanned a nine-month period. The latest entry was from February 2011, only two weeks earlier. Four pages, hardly a novel. A short story maybe?

Or real?

The thought made my stomach lurch and my throat close. I switched the machine off, my hand trembling a little. Stupid. Just some sad bloke's sick fantasy. But like sand in an oyster shell the notion stuck. It grated on me while I tried to paint, making it impossible to concentrate.

I haven't picked up a brush since.

That evening I sat in front of the television flicking through the channels. Nothing held my attention. The memory stick crouched at the edge of my vision, a shiny black carapace, like a malevolent beetle or a cockroach. I decided then there was one way to stop the flights of fancy. I just needed to prove to myself that the accounts were fictional.

Sept 24th 2010
She never locks up when she goes next door for the morning paper. I hid in the spare room all day. The excitement was unbearable, delicious. And then I waited while she cooked herself a meal and bathed and watched television. It was after midnight before she turned out the lights. She'd been drinking whisky, I could smell it on her breath and from the glass beside her. I thought it would make her drowsy but she flinched when I touched her and struggled and almost ruined everything. She made me angry. I had to punish her. After all, it could have been perfect. She had robbed me of that. She soon learnt her lesson and then I did it and the spasms started; the life bucking from her. I felt her go cold.

Then we were even. I still laid her out nicely, enjoyed her till the sun rose. Not long enough. With her spoiling it like that I had to cover my tracks. Everyone has candles around these days and some people forget to replace the smoke alarm batteries. Whisky's an accelerant. I want the next one to be perfect even if it takes me longer to find her.

I re-read the entries and made a note of the dates. There were no names or addresses, not even locations but I reckoned I could check those dates – for deaths. I looked online first, found the Office of National Statistics site. But their records only went up to the year 2009 and there were practically half a million deaths a year. That's getting on for ten thousand a week. Without more details there was no way to find out about a specific death on a particular date.

Oct 5th 2010
Every day, going about my business, knowing that what I am sets me apart. I have gone beyond the boundaries and reaped the rewards. If anyone could bottle this and sell it they'd make a killing (hah!).

I tried the local Record Office next. They had registered deaths for 2010 on microfiche. It took me several trips, booking the viewers for a couple of hours at a time. I started by eliminating all the men and then anyone under fifteen and over forty. Arbitrary I know, but I had to narrow it down somehow. And I focused on Manchester. After all, he'd been to the airport and he mentions the Metrolink when he talks about the third victim.

Dec 11th 2010
She got on at Cornbrook. It was like recognising someone. I followed her home. I can't wait – though I will. The anticipation makes it hard to think straight.

Even then I still had lists with dozens of deaths for each of the two dates in 2010. It was hopeless.

Danny rang the following week. Had I retired? Or was I just being even more lazy than usual? A virus, I told him, couldn't shake it off. So I hadn't got anything for him.

It became harder to sleep. The Wolf stalked my dreams. I thought about pills but that frightened me more. If he did come and I was comatose, I might never wake up. I tried to imagine what he'd done to the women. He was never explicit in what he wrote.

I spent a fortune on increased security. I could have gone to the police then, I had rehearsed a cover story about finding the laptop, but I feared the police would dig deeper. Want to know how I'd paid for my flat when I hadn't had any employment for over two years. They'd only have to check my bank records to see I handled a lot of cash. They were bound to be suspicious. I could end up in court for no good reason. In prison. So I delayed – hoping to find out it was all invented.

Jan 7th 2011
Tomorrow I'll be with her. This has been a long time coming, tricky with her going away so often. But now she's back. She'll soon be mine.

More than once I considered destroying the memory stick but what if it was all true and The Wolf was a killer, then this was proof. In one dream the memory stick was missing, I searched the flat in a frantic panic and woke up, drenched in sweat. The fear forced me from my bed to check that I still had it. I copied it to my own machine for back-up.

I stopped going to bed. The doctor suggested sleeping pills but I lied and said that side of things was fine, I just needed something for my anxiety during the daytime. He prescribed Prozac. It didn't help. But they say it takes a while to have any effect. As it turned out, I didn't have that long.

Jan 8th 2011
I was all ready but she brought a man home and he stayed with her. I'd been looking forward to it so very much. Everything focused, con-

centrated. I won't let her ruin it. I will not get angry. I won't give up either. She's the next one. No matter how long it takes.

Then I thought about trying the newspapers. Central Library was closed for refurbishment and they'd moved the archive to the Record Office so I went back there and trawled the newspapers they had on microfiche for the dates of the first two entries. June 12th 2010 had been a Saturday. Tucked away inside the following Monday's *Evening News* there was a paragraph headed *UNTIMELY DEATH*. My pulse raced and my stomach contracted as though I'd been thumped.

The story identified her as Janet Carr, 37, an administrator who was discovered by friends when she failed to turn up for a social engagement and didn't answer her phone. Miss Carr was a chronic asthmatic. There were no suspicious circumstances. The only reason her death was in the paper was the fact that Miss Carr was administrator of a charity involved in raising money for asthma research. It made good copy. Human interest.

I sat there in front of the microfiche reader, staring at the screen, feeling nauseous and the horror of it creeping across my skin like a rash. There was no mention of foul play. I'd imagined The Wolf strangling them but whatever he'd done, he'd done it in a way that avoided detection. Poisoning? Gassing? How else could he have killed and left it looking natural? Something to aggravate Janet Carr's asthma? Had he known she was asthmatic? Were the others? What else could he have used? I'd no idea.

I swapped that microfiche for the September one; the woman he had punished for flinching. It didn't take me long to find her. *Tragic Blaze Kills Nurse*. Fiona Neeson, 24, a nurse at Wythenshawe Hospital. An address in Sale. A spokesman for the Fire Service urged everyone to check their smoke alarms and to be aware of the very real hazards associated with candles in the home. This was a preventable death, he said.

The newspapers for 2011 hadn't been put onto the system yet.

When I came out of the library the bright light made me giddy, my knees buckled and I had to hold onto a lamppost till it passed.

Jan 10th 2011

*Each time I reach a higher level. The intensity is impossible to describe.
As if I'm able to fly, go anywhere, do anything. I can. I am. What else
is there? Nothing else comes anywhere close. She watched me. Her
eyes flew open as she felt it but she didn't move. No scream, no begging, just those wide, wild eyes and then her body took over and her
eyes rolled back in her head while she started dancing. She was marvellous. And I was even better than before. I never really knew what
joy was. Superb, sublime. I stayed until dawn. Those precious hours.
Felt like shouting from the rooftops. My dancing queen.*

How had he killed them?

At home I tried the internet. I found myself at sites covering topics as diverse as assisted suicide, medical negligence and
armed revolution. Surfing in the company of rednecks, crimi-
nologists, surgeons and serial killer fans. Anything remotely
useful I cut and pasted. I had also made photocopies of the
relevant articles from the newspaper microfiche and read and
re-read them hoping to find something that helped me make
sense of the whole affair.

Jan 11th 2011

*All day I relive it. Feel the thrill singing through my veins, every sense
heightened, each memory like a snapshot: the terror in her stare, the
grating noise of her last breath, the final tremors, the rhythm of her
dance of death, long limbs jerking so fiercely. I'm put in mind of surf-
ers, the ones who ride the big one. On top of the world. Invincible.*

I was scared. I no longer ate. The textures felt all wrong. I'd take
a mouthful and it would turn to dust or slime in my mouth.

Feb 20th 2011

*The hunger is growing again, already. But I cannot risk it yet. I close
my eyes and see her, the last one and it's the best trip in the world.
To hell and back. Myself in her eyes. The last hopeless suck of breath.
Body twitching and jolting. I can't stop. How could I ever stop. This is
my life now. Rich beyond dreams.*

Then I caught a news item, a young woman found dead in her Levenshulme flat had been identified as Kate Cruickshank. Don't ask me how I knew. I switched the television off but I couldn't get rid of the tension, my guts were knotted and I had an awful sense of foreboding.

I fell asleep in my chair. In my dream The Wolf came and I ran and locked myself in the shower room. I leant back against the door to catch my breath and there he was reflected in the mirror. I was trapped. Waking with awful pains in my chest and my heart hammering, I knew I had to go to the police.

My timing was shot at. I planned to go at lunchtime, imagining that people would be taking lunch breaks and coming and going, and I could just leave it all on the doorstep without being noticed. The laptop and the memory stick. Enclose an anonymous note telling them about The Wolf, about Janet Carr and Fiona Neeson and a woman whose name I didn't know who had died around January 10th. Tell them to investigate Kate Cruickshank.

There wasn't any doorstep. I walked past the place a couple of times and realised if I left it outside on the pavement someone could take it and The Wolf would carry on. Killing women. Haunting me.

So, I went in through the glass doors. There was no one at the desk in the small foyer, I placed the laptop on the counter and was turning to go when a policeman came out of the door behind.

'Miss?'

I began to walk away.

'Is this your bag, Miss?'

'No,' I moved more quickly. Ahead of me the doors clicked shut and then an alarm began to sound. I wheeled round in time to see the man disappear.

They thought it was a bomb.

Steel shutters began to roll down the glass frontage and I could see people evacuating the building from other exits, racing to cross the street. The alarm was deafening and then voices began shouting at me over the intercom. It was hard to hear above the din.

'It's just a laptop,' I yelled. 'Lost property.' The sirens continued to whoop and screech. I went and grabbed the laptop, looked up at the CCTV camera in the corner. 'Look,' I yelled, unzipping the case, opening the cover, so they could see, lifting out the anonymous note I'd left.

There was a hissing sound, and smoke and a peculiar smell and it was hard to breathe. My eyes were streaming, I was choking.

I wasn't Miss Popularity.

Once the Bomb Squad had stepped down and the building was re-opened I was taken to a small interview room and waited with a woman officer until a man came to take my details. He was a short, skinny man with chapped lips. There was an order to the paperwork which he stuck to rigidly. Having established my name, address, date of birth, nearest living relative (none) and occupation (unemployed artist), he finally let me talk.

While I explained about 'finding' the computer on the Metro and that it contained accounts of a series of murders, that the dates tallied with actual deaths in Manchester, his expression changed from weary to wary, then hardened. He hated me.

'Read it,' I urged.

'It could be a journalist's – research.'

That took me aback. I thought for a moment. 'No facts or figures, no names or addresses. I'm sure it's a diary. And the deaths have never been seen as murders – so what are they investigating? Just read the memory stick.'

'It was destroyed, along with the computer.'

'What?' I was appalled.

'Procedure.'

But there was still hope, 'I made a back-up file, it's at home on my machine. I've copies of newspapers too, they match the accounts.'

He still didn't seem to believe a word I said. 'How long have you had it?'

'A couple of days,' I lied. How could I explain I'd held onto it for nearly a month?

'You found this on Tuesday?'

'Yes, on the tram. The man who lost it, I can describe him, he got off at Mosley Street.' I gave him a description of The Wolf.

'And you were going?'

'To the Lowry.'

He rose without speaking, hitched his trousers up, left the room.

'Could I have a cup of tea?' I asked the PC.

She shrugged.

I began to cry.

The skinny man came back and grilled me some more, all about where I'd got the laptop. He seemed angry. I stuck to my story.

Looking back, it was all very fractured. Surreal even. Everyone still treating me like the mad bomber. Then they asked me to accompany them to my house. Show them the file and the other information.

I felt sick and light-headed on the way. I couldn't remember when I'd last eaten and the petrol fumes and the smell of fast food grease on the air made me queasy. The traffic was terrible; it took us an hour to get there. The skinny man drove and the woman sat with me in the back.

At my flat it took a while to get in, with all the locks and that. I showed them the photocopies of the newspapers, and the back-up copy of *Accounts* on my laptop. They took me into the kitchen. I was shivering even though it was so close. I could never get warm anymore. The woman poured me a glass of water but it tasted filthy.

There were more voices in the living room and a little hubbub of excitement in the interchange. At last, I thought, they were taking me seriously.

The Wolf came into my kitchen.

I knocked over my water in panic, scrambled to my feet, screaming, 'That's him, that's the man, it's his diary.'

Someone grabbed my arms and pinned them behind me. Someone else tried to calm me down.

The Wolf raised his eyebrows and lifted his hand. He held a small plastic bag, inside was a syringe.

'Not very well hidden,' his voice was soft.

'That's not mine,' I yelled. 'I am not a junkie.' I turned to the woman holding me. 'Check my arms. I've never taken anything like that.'

'You slipped up, last time,' The Wolf said. 'Kate Cruickshank. We found the mark.' He held up the bag again. Gave a wolfish grin. 'Rebecca Colne, I am arresting you for the murder of Kate Cruickshank on …'

I didn't hear the end of the caution. The room spun then dimmed. I passed out.

They gave me four life sentences. They tried me for four murders. The third one, she was Alison Devlin. She was two months pregnant.

The Metrolink had been closed the day I claimed to have seen the man leave the laptop and get off at Mosley Street: a system failure. When I told them the truth about the airport, they raised questions about my delay. Why wait so long? If I honestly thought this was information about a series of murders, why wait at all? I'd stolen the machine, I told them, I was frightened that I'd be prosecuted, I wanted to make sure it was true. None of my excuses made any difference. My change of story made them even more convinced I was responsible. And when I repeatedly claimed that the man who owned the laptop was one of the officers investigating me, they clearly thought me deranged.

They seized my own computer and found all the other files. All the internet junk I'd copied: methods of murder. My defence counsel argued about the dates, demonstrating that I'd downloaded stuff long after the first three murders, but I could see the jury turning against me. Looking at me sideways. I was told not to make accusations about The Wolf, it wouldn't help my case. They linked me to Fiona Neeson. We'd been members at the same gym. It was news to me.

The clincher was the DNA evidence. A hair of mine at the scene of Kate Cruickshank's death. It didn't matter that I'd never been there. Someone had – with a hair of mine, or dropped it into the forensics lab. That coupled with the syringe 'recovered' from my flat.

Juries love forensics, ask anyone. Never mind about logic or witnesses or other evidence – a bit of sexy science has them frothing at the mouth. Clamouring for conviction.

Like quicksand the more I struggled for the truth the deeper I sank. Till I was swallowing mud day after day in the courtroom. The weight of it crushing my lungs.

A stream of acquaintances and people I barely knew were wheeled out to attest to my controlling, cold and dubious character. The prosecution harped on about my lonely and dysfunctional upbringing, my isolation, my prior mental health problems. They held up my severe weight loss, my Prozac use, my insomnia as evidence of a guilty conscience. And my stunt at the police station as a cry for help. They never had a motive. How could they? I was a psychopath, I had a personality disorder – no motive required.

After the conviction, much was made of my lack of remorse and even more of the word murderess. The female of the species and all that.

They've turned down my application for an appeal. No new evidence. And no hope of being considered for parole until I admit my guilt.

Maybe I'm safer in here. The bars, the locks, the cameras. If they let me out he'd be waiting, wouldn't he? Lips slightly parted, hair slicked back, those lupine teeth. Waiting to get me once and for all. The sting of the syringe as he inserts the needle. The dull ache as he presses the plunger, forcing the air into a vein. The seconds left as the bubble speeds around my bloodstream. Zipping along as if in a flume. An embolism. Fizzing through my heart and on into my lung – tangling with my blood vessels. Making me gasp, claw for air. A jig of death. Stopping everything. Blowing me away.

Margaret Murphy

Act of Contrition

What she's doing is wrong – she knows it – she has lied and lied and lied. And she's about to do far worse. She's been spending hours – days even – on the forum, checking who's signed in, monitoring the threads, starting discussions of her own. But she would never say that those hours had been wasted. Sometimes he lurks at the edges, checking out the chat without signing in, so she has to post a comment, trying to think of things that might interest him, hoping that he'll private message her – anything for the chance to make contact. He fills her every waking moment – her dreams are all of him – he's become an obsession, she knows that. But there's nothing she can do about it. And today – *right now* – she is minutes away from seeing him, and she knows that the moment will make everything right.

But what if I've made a mistake? The internet is dangerous, everyone's always saying it, and it's true, so she has arranged to meet him at Costa Coffee in the High Street. Plenty of opportunity to check him out, and the option to walk out the door, don't look back.

Or take the next step. *The next step!* One hand flutters to her mouth. *What are you thinking? Do you want this? I mean, really?*

He suggested they meet – private messaging her on the forum:

–Meet me, he'd said. A command, an order, not a plea.

–I don't know. It's a sin, what we're doing. She believes in goodness and evil, in virtue and sin.

–We're just talking.

–Are we?

–For now ;-)

–I'm serious.

The forum was quiet that night, and his answers had been coming through fast, but this time he took a while to respond.

—Define sin.

Her answer was prompt, she didn't even need to think about it.

—Breaking a moral rule.

—Rules're for schools. Rules're for fools. Rules're for people with no imagination.

This rankled.

—I have imagination!

But what she sees in her imagination is terrible — awful — and this becomes one more secret she must keep, even from him. Especially from him.

—Hey, I didn't mean *you*. He comes back — he seems a bit sorry for being so sharp. So smart-arsed.

—I'm talking about parents, grownups. They make you stick to their rules, and the trouble with rules is they only work in straight lines.

It's a perfect day: sunny, warm. He can even smell fresh-cut grass above the diesel-whiff of traffic on the ring road. *Maybe I'll take her down by the river, stop for a picnic.* He's brought two chilled bottles of WKD Vodka Blue — because she said that's her favourite. They're sweating in his rucksack, on the seat beside him, jostling and singing out as the bus rides the pot-holes into town. The day couldn't promise anything more wonderful: him and GeekGirl and two bottles of WKD.

That's what she calls herself, 'GeekGirl'. Her avatar is a studious-looking manga with thick-rimmed glasses; his is a flop-haired boy, carrying a guitar. GeekGirl's alias is what attracted him in the first place: kind of self-aware, but with a knowing humour. His handle is Wolfboy, on account of the lycanthropes in *Twilight* — ironically, it's the outsiders who are more interested in the lycans — the girls with the pack instinct go for the vampy types. Wolfboy prefers the outsiders, the girls who stand out — stand *apart* — from the rest.

He loves the internet's distance and its intimacy. You could be anywhere in the world, but a private chat room can feel cosier than your own bedroom because – well – because often you *are* in your own bedroom, on your own turf, just like they are. So it feels like you're having a conversation, face-to-face, without all the confusing non-verbal signals and demands for instantaneous reactions. He's never been that good in social situations: in real-time, what he says never sounds the way it did in his head – not as clever, or as witty – in all honesty, sometimes, it doesn't even make sense. But as Wolfboy, he can take as long as he needs to think about what he really means to say. In virtual-time, nobody sees you typing, deleting, typing again, sweating over the words. They only see the final, per-fected phrase, after you hit the send key.

A ripple of sound from his mobile: he has a new text mes-sage.

–Where U @?

He feels a thrill to the bone, despite her annoying use of abbreviations and symbols. He's uncomfortable with the lan-guage of texts: the forum insists on standard English, text slang and abbreviations are banned, and he's slightly irritated that she has addressed him so tersely. But this isn't the forum, and anyway, he's willing to accept the downside of text communi-cation for the chance to meet GeekGirl.

–Bus, he texts. He can be terse, too.

–OK. CU l8tr.

–See you later! he texts back, spelling out the words, hoping she'll sense his disapproval of txt lingo.

She had made the first move, a few weeks ago. She'd sent him a private message, asking for his real name.

–Meet me and I'll tell you.

She was quiet for a bit, and he could almost *see* her, chewing her lip, trying to make up her mind.

–A/S/L?

This was a question – or technically three: Age/ Sex/ Location? You're not supposed to share personal stuff. He evaded an answer by pointing out her breach of the forum rules.

–It's a PM, she'd replied. –Who's gonna know?

So GeekGirl was willing to break the rules. Promising. He answered her question with a question:

–Why the sudden interest?

–Just want to be sure you're not some crusty, perving for teens.

'Crusty' – synonymous with wrinkly, old-arse, croc face, coffin dodger. *Like she doesn't fancy 'old'.*

–Come on, GeekGirl – what about Edward Cullen? he'd demanded. Their virtual meeting place is a forum on one of the hundreds of *Twilight* fan-sites; in the story, Bella Swan, a teen, falls for Edward Cullen, a vampire six times her age.

–If we're drawing parallels, he went on, Cullen is old enough to be Bella Swan's *ancestor*.

–Ah, but Edward Cullen *was* a teen when he turned vamp, and he doesn't *look* old. And what with those gorgeous golden eyes and a fabulous body and – let's face it, his all round, all over, *completely*, one hundred per cent bee-yoo-tiful body, a girl could forgive a lot.

He waited a while, to let her know she'd hurt his feelings. Then he gritted his teeth and typed and deleted and typed again, came up with:

–AGE: Well, I'm not a hundred and four. SEX: Male – hence Wolf*boy*, not Wolf*bitch*. He didn't get as far as LOCATION. She replied in a short second, mistyping in her rush to apologise.

–Oh, Wolfboy! Please dont be mad – I dind't mean to hurt your feelings.

This was good: if she'd taken her time, or come back all snippy – or worse, logged off – he'd've de-friended her from his list, dumped her, and moved on. But she was sorry and sweet, and told him that she was just trying to be careful, like the manual said.

–Wait – there's a manual?

–Haven't you read it? It's called Trust No One ;-)

He liked the smiley emoticon – it showed she was trying hard to make amends.

He sent her one in return – the eyeroller, to let her know she didn't have to be that way with him, and so she'd know they were friends again.

–Anyway... She didn't type anything else for a few minutes, the teasing, trying to make out she'd gone all shy on him, maybe wanting him to draw her out. He held off, and eventually a fresh message popped up in his inbox. A confession:

–I'm nothing like Bella, either, she said.

He smiled as he typed:

–Oh, I hope not.

She took that as a compliment, but what he meant was, Bella's seventeen. *That's way too old.*

GeekGirl, on the other hand, is fourteen. Likes: the colour purple, science, Fergie, Fyfe Dangerfield, Miley Cyrus and *Twilight* (of course). Hates: football, vamp wannabes, brussel sprouts and Justin Beiber (–He's such a boy!).

He lists Scouting for Girls among his likes. She got all excited over that, said she knew they were on the same psychic plane. *She thinks I mean the band.*

–Their lyrics express what I feel in my heart, she wrote.

Their lyrics express insecurity, ambivalence, fear, anxiety, and rebelliousness – everything an average teen feels in her heart, so he says:

–Yeah, they're totally *real*.

It's a five-minute walk from the bus station. His heart seems to want to race ahead of him, it's beating so hard against his ribcage. He feels the bottles in his rucksack, jittering against his back, the steadier weight of the digital camcorder. It cost a bit extra for the Sony, but it was worth it, for the full HD, 5.1 surround sound, and superb freeze-frame and still capabilities.

Nine forty-five, and Costa is heaving. He hooks a thumb through the shoulder strap of his rucksack and ruffles his hair a bit before he pushes the door open. He sees a young mum, sharing a fruit smoothie with her toddler, two pensioners feeding gloop to a baby in a pram; a fat girl, staring unhappily at her own reflection in the window; a posse of builders chatting up the barrista, plaster dust on their faces and their steel-capped boots; a skinny woman, all cheekbones and close-cropped hair. She's got a laptop open in front of her, mobile phone glued to her ear. She stares through him, intent on a discussion of sales figures and spreadsheets, like she was in her own office.

But where is GeekGirl?

He notices the blimp watching him. She looks away quickly, but there's no mistaking the ache of longing in her eyes.

Fuck, no. He can't decide if he's more outraged or angry. *Call Trading Standards – I want to sue for false representation.* He walks to her table with a deliberate swagger. She fidgets and blushes, looks like she'd like to fly out of the place, or melt like the tub of lard she is and sink through the cracks in the floorboards. He bends, pushing his face so close to hers that she has no choice but to look at him.

'Not in a million years, darling.'

His phone vibrates in his hand, and with it, the familiar wave of sound that tells him he has a text message. He glances briefly at the screen, keeping his face close enough to smell the fat girl's perfume: JLo, and triple chocolate muffin.

–Where RU?

It's from GeekGirl. *Where am I?* The muffin girl is staring into her coffee, fat tears rolling down her fat cheeks, and feels a tiny spark of hope.

–Coffee shop, like we said. You?

–School.

She's stood him up. He should be mad, but he looks again at the fat girl and laughs from sheer relief.

He moves toward the door, thinking how he should reply, but a text comes through, faster than he can text, faster – almost – than he can think.

–Mum knows.

Shit.

–How could she know?

–How do mothers know ANYTHING? She's got X-ray friggin eyes – she just KNOWS when I'm lying. She ALWAYS knows.

Okay...This is just panic, last minute nerves. He knows how to deal with this.

–It just feels like that. You need to relax,

Before he can get to the end of the sentence, she's sent another text:

–She drove me 2 school. Wdnt leave till I went in. What shd I DO?

–Stay calm.

–Wel, thx for the advice, but I'd have to BE calm 2 STAY calm!

Cheeky bitch. Attitude is something he can do without.

–Okay, we'll call it off.

–Wolfboy PLS! I don't know what 2 do!

Worth one last try? If he plays it right, she'll be so sorry for being a bitch, she'll be extra nice.

–Look, GeekGirl, it's your life. How do you want to spend it – your way, or hers?

–But if Im caught...

No apostrophe. I really will have to talk to her about her punctuation.

–Tell them you have a hospital appointment. They'll never suspect GeekGirl. I mean, how much time have you had off school this year, anyway?

–None.

–Well, there you go.

It takes her five minutes to get back to him. When she does, she's already on the way. She gives him directions to her school. It has 'Saint' in the name. It's the other side of town, will take him twenty minutes to walk it, but a convent school girl – in school uniform. *Oh, boy...*

He sees her from across the street; she's leaning against the school wall, texting on her mobile, the hood of her jacket pulled up. She's wearing a grey pleated skirt, the hem a modest three inches above the knee, black shoes, knee-length white socks. She's *tiny*.

Pinch me, I must be dreaming.

His phone trills in his pocket. He takes his eyes off her for a second, no more, but when he looks again, she's gone. He feels a stab of alarm, a sick dread that he's missed his chance.

He looks again at the screen. *GeekGirl, thank God.* He opens the message, but there's no text. He frowns, crosses the street at a trot, passes the side gate, almost misses the alley off to the left, behind the school's boundary wall. She's up ahead, walking fast, light on her feet. He calls after her, but she keeps on going. He breaks into a jog, the drinks bottles ringing like a klaxon in his rucksack.

At the precise moment that he is ready to give up, she slows her pace and pauses next to a row of dumpsters. He stops for breath, bending to gulp in air.

She reaches behind and gives her skirt a naughty little flick with her fingers and he catches a glimpse of white panties.

He groans, hitches his rucksack higher onto his sweating back and sees her dart out of sight behind the dumpsters.

He moves forward, the soles of his shoes slapping heavily on the cobbles, passing a door in the high brick wall. It must lead to the kitchen courtyard: he hears the clank of metal implements, the air is thick with the smell of over-boiled cabbage and steamed fish. Friday, convent school – one that observes the old traditions.

The dumpsters reek of rotting food – surely she doesn't want to do it here? But if that's what rattles her rosary, he's not the man to deny her. She giggles, and he feels it like she's run her fingernails down his spine.

She's going nowhere and he's in no hurry, so he shrugs off his pack and sets it on the ground, fishes out the camcorder and takes a panning shot.

He walks slowly past the first two dumpsters, his heart pounding. The excitement of anticipation is so fine, he decides to play it out a little longer, using the viewfinder as his eyes, working from her shoes up.

Lord save us – they're patent leather with a narrow strap across the instep. His heart is pounding in his ears, his hands are slick, and he's already hard. *Baby, I'm about to rock your world.* He's looking at slim ankles in those dazzling white socks, a band of smooth, tanned flesh between the top of the sock and the hem of the skirt. He focuses for a tantalising second on her thighs, on the sliver of shadow cast by her skirt hem, before continuing his tracking shot. Her jacket is unzipped to the waist, her shirt open to show a hint of white bra lace. He lingers a moment, glad of the Sony's anti-shake technology. He pans up, but she closes her hand over his. His whole body resonates with desire, pulsing to the rush of blood in his ears.

'Look at me,' she says, her voice husky.

He tears his gaze from the image in the viewfinder. Her face is in shadow, and she reaches up to pull the jacket hood back.

This isn't right.

He can't make sense of what he sees. *This isn't GeekGirl.*

She smiles at him and he feels sick. This just is not *right*.

GeekGirl is fourteen years old. This is someone twenty years older. Her hand snakes out, gripping the back of his neck.

He grabs the hand, tries to prise it off his skin, but she's strong – much stronger than she looks.

'What's up, Wolfboy?' she asks. 'Don't you like women your own age?'

Horrified, he stares into her face and sees another – much younger.

'Misty?'

'Misty,' she says, 'is dead.'

He feels a pressure in his groin, then a rush of wetness and heat. She steps away and for some reason, he crumples to his knees. The camcorder is suddenly too heavy to lift; it records a pool of dark liquid on the ground, spreading in a slow tide around him. She takes the recorder from his hand.

'Here,' she says, 'let me – it'd be a shame to miss this.'

❖

He takes ten minutes to die. She had severed his femoral vein, slicing lengthways to increase the bleed, because this was how her daughter chose to end her life. Within hours of her posting it online, the clip is listed as the top video on YouTube, VirginMedia and MSN. It stays there for twenty-four hours, until a public outcry forces its removal.

Janice Tregarron places her shoulder bag onto the ground. It has rained all morning, but the sun now dazzles on the footpaths, and the pathways and the damp earth of the cemetery are steaming, exhaling a gauzy mist that spills into the hollows and swirls around the gravestones. From the bag Janice takes a metal bowl, lighter fluid, matches, and a diary. Janice is a Catholic; she finds comfort in the order and mystery of its rituals, but this is no religious sacrament. This is a purging.

She sets out the items in front of her daughter's grave. Janice tears each page out, one by one, twists it and places it into the metal bowl. When every page is accounted for, she squirts some of the lighter fuel onto the mound and drops a lighted match onto it. The diary catalogues ten meetings between Alison, known on the forums as Misty, and Keith Grant, aka Wolfboy. Her daughter, naive, but no fool, discovered and documented his true name. In the earlier entries, Alison believes she is in love, but by the tenth, she is suicidal. Her classmates discovered video recordings of her with Wolfboy online. Neither was named, and Wolfboy hid his face, but Alison was easily identifiable. The images were explicit and distasteful. The girls tormented her. It began with name-calling, but quickly escalated: images of her and Wolfboy taped inside her locker, her desk, condoms stuffed in the pockets of her coat while it hung in the cloakroom, a dildo, left on her seat in the classroom. They spat on her as she ran the gauntlet of the corridors between lessons; they shoved and slapped her as she queued for lunch, tripped her on the stairs, and elbowed and kicked her on the sports field. She received phonecalls, texts and emails, but worst of all – the thing that finally broke her – they posted her email address and mobile phone number, together with one of the most explicit photographs, online, advertising free sex.

Keith Grant had made no attempt to hide the fact that he was recording her. But she'd believed him when he said he wanted to remember always how beautiful she was and how sexy their first days together had been.

Janice found Alison's diary three months after her daughter's suicide. She could not believe that she didn't know her daughter was in such distress. And the moment she thought it, the signs, the moments of almost-revelation, the half-spoken confessions, the unspoken pleas to be understood, crowded into her consciousness and she saw that she had failed as a mother and as a human being. Her business affairs had taken precedence over her daughter's welfare: she had noticed and discounted Alison's reluctance to get up for school, had replaced damaged uniform blouses and sports kit without comment, *too busy* to be bothered with questions, too tired to cope with the arguments that questions inevitably provoked. She had seen the marks on Alison's arms and legs, and had wilfully allowed herself to be persuaded that they were trophy bruises from hockey and netball.

It was all in the diary, every slap and punch and trip and shove and kick. She could have – *should have* – taken it to the police, but she chose not to. The justice system would have condemned Grant as a predator, a paedophile preying on young girls, but he would not have been tried for murder – even though he killed Alison just as surely as if he'd wielded the razor blade himself. So she used Alison's diary to lead her to Wolfboy; she trawled the forums, found him, lured him, and killed him. Janice Tregarron believes in goodness and evil, in virtue and sin, and heaven and hell. Some would say she had sought revenge, and perhaps they would be right: it's true that evil deeds had been punished, but there was no vengeful feeling in Janice's heart as she plunged the blade into Grant's femoral vein, no anger as she watched him die. Rather, it was an act of contrition, a plea for forgiveness.

She opens her purse and takes out the small blue SD card she'd taken from Grant/Wolfboy's camcorder. About a centimetre square, it is burdened with so much misery that Janice is amazed that it can weigh so little – light enough to balance on the tip of her finger. But encoded in the thin-layer technology of its integrated circuits is a graphic, horrifying record of other girls, some younger than Alison.

She holds the tiny electronic manifest of cruelty and human degradation over the flames until she cannot bear the heat any longer, then tilts her hand and the thin square of blue plastic tumbles into the fire.

Martin Edwards

The Case of the Musical Butler

In the months following my marriage, I remained in regular contact with Mr Sherlock Holmes, and ten days after he paid a welcome visit to our home, I took a week's holiday from my practice, and returned to the lodgings he and I had shared; my wife was visiting her mother, who was suffering from a minor indisposition. During this period, Holmes was consulted by Sir Greville Davidson with regard to his butler, but the circumstances of the case were so delicate that it remains impossible for my account of it to be published whilst the last of the principal characters in the little drama remains alive. Nevertheless, I have decided to write up my notes before memories fade, since the whole affair provides a remarkable insight into an unexpectedly compassionate side to Holmes' personality, as well as demonstrating his skill as a solver of puzzles.

Sir Greville entered our lives on a cold and blustery October afternoon. As I watched from the bow window as a brisk wind blew leaves across Baker Street, I noticed a tall man, limping along the pavement with the aid of a stout walking stick. I estimated that he was some sixty-five years of age, with craggy features and silver hair, and that he was a man of means, given the smartness of his black frock coat and grey trousers, and the shine of his shoes. As he examined the numbers of the houses, I described him to my friend.

'I suppose that will be Sir Greville Davidson from Oaklands Hall, on the outskirts of Wallingford,' Holmes murmured absently, 'I anticipated that he might wish to seek my advice.'

'Holmes, you astound me!' I exclaimed. 'In London alone, there must be scores of men who match the description I supplied. How can you possibly assert...?'

Holmes yawned. 'It is of no consequence, Watson. Besides, I may very well be mistaken.'

For Sherlock Holmes to admit a possible flaw in one of his deductions – even when proffered in such casual fashion and on the basis of the slenderest evidence – was a sign that he had become gripped by *ennui*. This I found disturbing, for I knew, none better, that in order to alleviate boredom, he was apt to reach for the morocco case in which he kept his syringe and cocaine.

The bell clanged, and when Mrs Hudson flourished a card and announced that Sir Greville Davidson wished to see Holmes, I was about to offer my congratulations on the inspired nature of his guesswork – for what else could it have been? – when my friend murmured, 'Send him away.'

'Holmes!' I expostulated. 'You cannot simply decline to see the man!'

'Pray, why not?' Holmes lifted his right eyebrow, as if he lacked the energy to raise both. 'I crave the stimulation of an unorthodox and knotty problem. I am a consulting detective, not a nursemaid to the gentry.'

'And how can you be sure that Sir Greville does not wish to seek your advice on a matter of breath-taking complexity?'

Holmes waved a hand at the sheaf of clippings which lay on his roll-top desk. 'Because bloodstained clothes, apparently belonging to a tramp, have been found in a ditch near the Thames outside Wallingford. Of the hypothesised tramp, there is no sign, and the police's lack of concern appears to border on lack of interest, but an excitable journalist with nothing better to write about has penned a paragraph raising the spectre of foul play. If my memory of the geography of Oxfordshire does not fail me, the discovery was made adjacent to the boundary of the Oaklands Estate, one of the most notable in the county. If a crime has perchance been committed, Sir Greville is unlikely to be interested in identifying the perpetrator. He withdrew from society some years ago, as I recall, and a man in his position is apt, in such a case, to think only of protecting his reputation and privacy. Assisting the wealthy to keep their names out of the Press is, however, a task for others.'

The long-suffering landlady cast a despairing glance in my direction, but knew better than to argue with her lodger when he was in such a humour. Scarcely did she leave the room, however, than the door was flung open again, and the gentleman whom I had seen in Baker Street appeared before us. His face was red with the exertion of climbing the stairs, and his brow glistened with perspiration. The look in his gray eyes betrayed a deep anxiety.

'Mr Holmes, I must apologise for disturbing you in such an unseemly fashion, but I must speak to you!'

My friend frowned. 'Sir Greville, I fear that...'

'For pity's sake!' the intruder exclaimed. 'I am at my wits' end! Will you not allow me five minutes to explain the circumstances that bring me here?'

A curious look passed across Holmes' face and I saw that, although it was out of character for him to change his mind on such a matter, our visitor's evident anguish had made an impression upon him.

'Five minutes, Sir Greville? Very well. Are we agreed that, as soon as that time has expired, you will take your leave upon my indicating that I wish to hear nothing more?'

I could not conceive that our visitor was accustomed to being addressed in so forceful, and indeed humiliating, a manner, but he nodded by way of assent.

'Very well.' Holmes leaned forward, and I sensed that his interest was quickening, as if Sir Greville had passed an unspoken test. 'Pray be seated and explain to Dr Watson and myself what brings you here.'

'Mr Holmes, you will be aware that my family has lived at Oaklands Hall for generations. Almost one hundred and fifty years, to be precise. But I am the last of the line. My dear wife and I had two sons, but the elder died of consumption when he was nine years old, and the younger within two days of his birth. The difficulties that my wife suffered in labour meant that we were never able to have any further children, and I reconciled myself to the prospect of dying without an heir. Our consolation was a very happy marriage, but some five years ago, my wife became unwell and the final years of her life were spent as an invalid. Because of her illness, I had time enough to prepare for bereavement, but since her death in January, my life has been empty, and frankly I shall not be sorry when the time comes for the two of us to be reunited.'

The old man hesitated, as if overcome by emotion, and I saw Holmes cast a weary glance at the clock on the mantelpiece. Time was running short for Sir Greville to command my friend's attention.

'Mr Holmes, some eighteen months ago, I engaged the services of a butler by the name of Meade. His predecessor had served my family for thirty years, but died suddenly of a heart attack. I have always placed high store on the quality of my servants, and my wife was attended by a trained nurse as well as a companion. Meade was a young man with limited experience, but came with an excellent character from the house in the North of England where he had worked previously.'

'As a butler?'

'For a few months, yes. Apparently he had started as a man-servant, employed by a brother and sister named Drake, but had shewn such devotion to duty that he earned rapid promotion. Miss Drake spoke most highly of him, and emphasised that he would have remained in their employment had she and her brother not decided to move to the Continent. Their loss, she assured me, would be my gain.'

'And you took her at her word?'

'Mr Holmes, I am old enough and cynical enough to be well aware that a glowing testimonial may be given by a person glad to be rid of its subject, but I fancy that I am a good judge of a fellow, and Meade impressed me as industrious and keen to learn. Nor was I disappointed. In a very short time, he proved himself indispensable, and his support was invaluable during the last difficult months of my wife's life. Since that time he has served me with absolute dedication and I have come to regard him – not as a friend, precisely, you will understand, but as a man in whom I may repose the utmost trust and confidence. No one could be more reliable, and if my boys had lived, I would wish them to have been as decent, hard-working and kindly as young Meade.' Breathing hard, Sir Greville mopped his brow with a monogrammed handkerchief. 'His constancy therefore makes the latest turn of events all the more astonishing.'

Holmes leaned forward. 'Pray continue.'

'What troubles me is that Meade has disappeared without a trace.'

'When was this?'

'I last saw him on Saturday night. I felt indisposed – Meade had himself walked all the way into the town that morning to purchase some medicines for me – and I retired very early, at six o'clock. He was not due to work on Sunday – that is, the day before yesterday – and I told him that if he wished to take himself off for the evening, that was perfectly in order.'

'And he has not as yet returned?' My friend yawned. 'There may, of course, be many explanations for a servant's failure to attend his place of work.'

Sir Greville's stern features creased in a frown and his eyes flashed. For an instant it was borne home to me that this man had once been far more formidable than the ageing and ailing individual ensconced in our sitting room.

'You have not heard the half of it, Mr Holmes. Let me assure you that Meade is the very soul of reliability. Never once has he failed in the slightest duty. He commands the respect of all my servants, and I can only say that I find him as attentive as he is accomplished.'

'And what, pray, are his particular accomplishments?' my friend enquired in a languid tone.

'He is very capable in all household duties. When my cook was taken ill some months ago, he deputised for her in the kitchen with rare skill. But more than that, he is a talented musician. When, shortly after he arrived at Oaklands, he mentioned that he enjoyed playing the pianoforte, I asked if he would play for my wife one day, expecting little more than a hammering-out of a few familiar tunes, but to my amazement I found that he could play Chopin exquisitely. Even in her final hours, my poor wife found a degree of solace in his skill, and for that alone I shall forever be in his debt. Since she died, I have often asked him to entertain me and he takes such evident pleasure in it, that I once asked him if he had not considered forging a career as a musician. However, he simply smiled and said that he would find large audiences too daunting. I found that quite credible, for despite his natural affability, Meade has always struck me as a person who is happiest in his own company. He would eschew the limelight.'

'Perhaps he has changed his mind and resolved to seek his fortune elsewhere,' my friend suggested.

'No, I cannot conceive of it, Mr Holmes. However, when he failed to return, I looked in his room and realised that he had taken with him his clothes and other possessions.'

'Did anyone see him leave the Hall?'

'I questioned my servants, but none of them could cast any light on the matter. He might have left at any time between six o'clock on Saturday evening, and half past eight the next morning. I caused enquiries to be made at the local station, and I learned that a person in a coat and muffler and carrying a suitcase had been seen catching a train to London. This was probably Meade, but it is impossible to be sure. It was apparent that everyone else at Oaklands shared my bewilderment at Meade's disappearance, which came utterly out of the blue. And then, this morning – I received the following missive.'

Our visitor plunged his hand into his pocket and extracted an envelope which he passed to Holmes. It was addressed, in a neat and curving script, to Sir Greville at Oaklands Hall, and my friend inspected it with as much care as if it were a manuscript written in cuneiform before sliding out a sheet of notepaper which bore a few words in the same careful hand.

Sir Greville,
I must apologise profoundly for the suddenness of my departure from your service. Suffice to say that I could not have wished for a better master, and I thank you for your many kindnesses from the bottom of my heart.
Yours sincerely,
M. Meade

'You see, Mr Holmes?' Sir Greville demanded. 'No explanation whatsoever.'

'You are aware, presumably, that certain items have been found in a ditch not far from your estate?' my friend asked.

Sir Greville nodded. 'Indeed, sir. Yesterday, a passing cyclist discovered certain items of bloodstained clothing in a ditch and informed the police. It has become a matter of some notoriety in the neighbourhood. But the clothes belonged to a tramp, Mr Holmes. It is inconceivable that Meade would ever wear ragged things.'

'He takes a pride in his appearance?'

'Most certainly. I have never known a man so neat in his attire. You may take it from me, sir, that the garments in the ditch have no connection with Meade.'

'And you wish me to find Meade?' Holmes asked, a curious note entering his voice.

'I do.' Sir Greville's voice trembled. He was, I surmised, a man unaccustomed to displaying weakness, but it was plain that he was close to tears. 'You see, I am a dying man, if my doctor is to be believed, and I wished to repay Meade for his selfless service to my wife and myself. I had it in mind to adopt him as my son and heir.'

Two hours later, Holmes rejoined me in the sitting room at 221b Baker Street, rubbing his hands together and shifting his armchair closer to the fire. Having despatched Sir Greville back to Oaklands Hall for a good rest, with an assurance that he would look into the matter of the disappearing butler, and call upon his client on the morrow, he had promptly disappeared himself, without a word of explanation.

'Well, Watson, what do you make of Sir Greville's tale?'

I cleared my throat before replying. I had not been idle during my friend's absence, and I had managed to make a deduction or two of my own.

'As it happens, I have fathomed why you expected his visit,' I announced. 'You had read a paragraph in the newspaper about the conundrum of the bloodstained clothing, and you inferred that the proximity of the find to Sir Greville's estate would prompt him to consult you. Quite elementary.'

'Very good, Watson!' Holmes clapped loudly. I was not unaware of a tinge of mockery in his response to my sharpness, but his jovial mood was at least a welcome contrast to the world-weariness that had preceded Sir Greville's arrival. 'And the story about Meade?'

'I fancy that, Sir Greville's belief notwithstanding, the clothing found in the ditch did belong to the butler. If he wished to leave Oaklands for some nefarious purpose, he may well have wished to disguise himself as a tramp. And thus clad, what if some other vagabond set upon him?'

'Killing Meade and tossing his garments into the ditch?'

'It is a plausible theory,' I said, nettled by the sardonic gleam in his eyes.

'Perhaps,' my friend said, in a tone that made it clear he thought otherwise. 'Of course, your supposition fails to explain the note from Meade.'

'A forgery,' I announced, with more confidence than I felt.

'A forgery by a vagabond who can imitate an elegant hand so as to deceive someone familiar with the author's writing?'

'Can you offer a better interpretation of the facts presented to us?' I retorted.

'My good fellow,' Sherlock Holmes said with a heavy sigh, 'have I not lectured you before on the folly of theorising without data? Evidence is what we seek, and evidence is precisely what I have been endeavouring to secure, with the assistance of those grubby young rascals who assist my enquiries every now and then.'

'Really? And what is the Irregulars' mission this afternoon?'

'I have sent them to Camden Town, of course.'

'Why Camden Town?'

Holmes uttered a low groan. 'Watson, did the Lord not give you eyes to see? The post-mark on the envelope containing Meade's note was from Camden Town.'

'So you believe Meade to be alive and hiding out in London?'

'I would not go so far as to say that,' Holmes said, and with characteristic indifference to my protestations, he refused to say another word on the subject for the remainder of the evening.

Holmes and I rose early on the morrow, and ten o'clock saw our carriage draw up outside the imposing entrance to Oaklands Hall. Sir Greville Davidson's ancestral home was a handsome yet rather stark Palladian mansion, nine bays wide and with a projecting portico. The surrounding estate was large and Holmes had insisted that our driver should follow a circuitous route passing by the ditch where the bloodstained garments had been discovered. It ran alongside a hawthorn hedge at the far extremity of the grounds of Oaklands Hall. Through gaps in the hedge, I glimpsed swans gliding across a small lake fringed by willow trees.

From the shuttered windows of the west wing, I surmised that Sir Greville made little use of a substantial portion of the Hall. An air of melancholy hung about the place, as though the life was ebbing from it, as well as from its master.

In the absence of the butler, a housemaid answered the door and led us directly through a vast entrance hall with elaborately carved door-cases to an octagonal study with views across to the Old Hall and the lake. Sir Greville was seated in one of three leather armchairs; behind him stood a writing desk and walls lined with shelves of calf-bound tomes. Our host's cheeks were pallid and even a man without my medical expertise was bound to observe that his health was deteriorating at an alarming rate. The disappearance of his favoured servant, less than a twelvemonth after the loss of his wife, was a blow he was finding impossible to withstand.

Struggling to his feet, he extended a hand in feeble greeting. 'Have you any news?' he asked.

Holmes shook his head. 'As yet, there is nothing more that I can tell you, Sir Greville, but there are certain questions that I would like to put.'

'Naturally.' Our host waved to the maid. 'Martha, please bring tea and refreshments for my guests.'

As the girl was about to leave the room, Holmes said to her, 'Martha, a moment of your time, if I may.'

The maid stopped in her tracks, blushing furiously.

'Sir?'

'How did you find Meade, the butler?'

Martha's shoulders seemed to be stiff with tension. She cast a quick glance at her employer, as if seeking permission to express an opinion. When he inclined his head a fraction, the girl breathed a little more easily, yet I fancied there was something equivocal in her expression. Some knowledge, perhaps, that she did not wish to share with Sir Greville.

'He... he is a very decent sort, sir. Of course, he kept himself to himself. It was rare for us to converse on a social footing.'

'You did not know him well?' Holmes asked.

Again the maid seemed to choose her words with care. 'No, I cannot claim that I knew Mr Meade well.'

She laid a curious emphasis on the name *Mr Meade*, but what – if anything – it signified, I could not tell, and within a moment she had scurried off to the kitchen, shutting the door behind her.

Sir Greville turned to Holmes. 'You wished to interrogate me, Mr Holmes?'

My friend bowed. 'A few questions only. First, could you provide me with a description of the butler?'

'He is a relatively short and slender man. I should say no more than five feet six inches in height. He has a thick mop of jet black hair, and a fresh and pleasant face, quite boyish. I doubt whether he is thirty years old, young for a butler, of course. As I have mentioned, he is always immaculately turned out.'

Holmes nodded thoughtfully. 'Second, did you by any chance retain the testimonial supplied to you by Miss Drake in respect of the butler?'

'As a matter of fact, I did.' Sir Greville hobbled to the writing desk, and his arthritic fingers fiddled awkwardly with a key before he managed to unlock one of the drawers. 'Here, you will see how highly she spoke of him.'

Holmes perused the reference, which was written in a spiky, sloping hand. Miss Emma Drake gave her address as Parkgate Hall in Wirral, and she had taken pains to heap praise upon the butler's qualities and love of hard work, even mentioning his love of music, as if to emphasise that a man with taste could be relied upon. In conclusion, she had, in gushing terms worthy of a flowery novelette, expressed her dismay that a move to Europe would deprive her brother Vernon and herself of Meade's services.

'Most interesting,' Holmes said warmly. I shot him a glance, as I saw nothing remarkable in the testimonial, and it was unlike my friend to utter platitudes, but his expression was imperturbable. 'Miss Drake certainly did her utmost to ensure that her butler found a new position.'

'Meade lived up to the high expectations she established,' Sir Greville said. 'I decided to make him my heir, Mr Holmes, because I felt that a man of his sensitivity and gifts deserved something better than a lifetime of service. I should say that, of course, I have ensured in my will that my obligations to my other servants, as well as to a number of charitable organisations to which my wife and I lent active support in happier times, are amply fulfilled.'

'But the house and the residue of your estate go to the butler?'

'Is that so shocking, Mr Holmes?' the old man asked. 'Simply because Meade is not a member of my social class?'

'By no means. Far better that such an estate devolves to the industrious and deserving than some idle good-for-nothing. On that, we are bound to agree. But no doubt the news would cause quite a furore in the district. For a butler to inherit a fortune is sensational indeed.'

'Certainly, and I was conscious that, after my passing, mischief-makers might suggest that Meade had somehow brought undue influence to bear upon me. With that in mind, I instructed my lawyer to take all possible precaution to ensure that no objection could properly be made to my testamentary dispositions, or to my proposal to adopt Meade as my son.'

'And has he done so?'

'He has in recent weeks been taking all necessary steps, Mr Holmes. Although at first he thought my decision lamentable and my judgement awry, over time I persuaded him that, with no close family of my own, I was acting with perfect propriety in bequeathing the bulk of my estate to a man who had done so much to ease the difficult last years of my wife and myself.'

'Is anyone else aware of the contents of your will?'

'I made no secret of my intentions. I meant to proceed with the formalities of adoption at the earliest possible moment.'

'And what did Meade say to your plans?'

'When I first broke the news to him – just a fortnight ago – he was astounded, as you might expect. Indeed, he sought repeatedly to dissuade me from my intended course. There could be no clearer sign of the fellow's innate decency. He is selfless, Mr Holmes, and of how many people can that be said?'

My friend murmured assent. 'It does seem extraordinary that a man should turn his back on such an inheritance.'

'Precisely, Mr Holmes!'

'Tell me, how did he occupy himself on the Sundays when he enjoyed time away from his duties? Did he entertain visitors, or go out to meet friends?'

'He is not a social animal, Mr Holmes. Despite his pleasant personality, he is reserved in the company of others, and from remarks that he has let slip, I believe that he was orphaned at an early age, and has no living relatives. He does not drink, or indulge in any of the vices that afflict servants and other members of the lower class with such deplorable regularity. As a general rule, he stayed in his room each Sunday, perhaps going out for a stroll around the grounds if the weather was not inclement. Otherwise, he would play the piano. He found it easy to occupy himself in solitude. In addition to his love of music, he is an avid reader.'

'Unusual for a butler,' my friend commented.

'Perhaps, but as I have endeavoured to explain, Meade is no ordinary butler.'

'I entirely agree with you, Sir Greville.'

'The over-riding question is,' our host said, with a surge of passion that suggested Holmes' nonchalant demeanour was not to his liking, 'what has happened to him?'

Sherlock Holmes leaned back in his armchair and closed his eyes for a few moments. 'There is in addition one further point on which I seek your clarification, Sir Greville.'

'Anything, sir!'

'Am I right in surmising that your butler's Christian name was Mark?'

The look of astonishment on the old man's face was answer enough.

It was typical of Mr Sherlock Holmes that he refused to discuss the case at all for the entire duration of our journey back to London. As soon as we reached Baker Street, he absented himself, saying merely that the data now in my possession should at least enable me to build the foundations of a credible explanation for the butler's disappearance.

I found myself as irked by my friend's insouciant manner as I was baffled by Meade's apparently calculated decision to flee from Oaklands Hall at the very moment when he seemed destined to inherit a fortune. I could not help thinking that there was more merit in my initial supposition – that Meade had the misfortune to fall victim to some itinerant rogue – than Holmes was willing to allow. Merely because a theory is based upon instinct rather than factual evidence, it is not necessarily mistaken. There are bound to be occasions when reasoning precedes proof. Holmes had sneered at my speculation that the note from Camden Town might be a forgery, but I reminded myself that forgers are criminals, who stoop to murder if the prize is sufficiently enticing. What if Meade had in his possession money or possessions of great value? Could Sir Greville be confident that nothing had been taken from the Hall? What if Meade was a fraudster and a thief who had met a deserved come-uppance? Warming to the idea, I told myself that the person described in Miss Drake's testimonial sounded too good to be true. Suppose a confederate had forged *that* note, as part of a plan whereby Meade would worm his way into service at the Hall as a prelude to staging a robbery. If Meade learned that his master proposed to leave the estate to him, he might wish to abandon his co-conspirator, a decision that risked provoking a fatal attack.

By the time that Holmes returned, it was growing dark outside. I had armoured myself against his scorn, but as ever, he took me unawares. The chill air had brought a flush to his cheeks, and there was no gainsaying the jubilation in his voice as he hailed me.

'Come, Watson! We leave at once for Chester.'

I stared at him. 'This evening? Chester must be nearly two hundred miles away. What can you hope to achieve by such a journey?'

'Tonight, nothing, but I have arranged accommodation for us at Sir Greville's expense in the heart of that splendid Roman city. And tomorrow, Watson, I expect to establish incontrovertibly the truth behind the disappearance of the butler who showed such excellent taste in manifesting a fondness for Chopin.'

Nothing could persuade my friend to reveal what he had discovered, and I contented myself with enjoying the journey up to Cheshire, and the comforts afforded by the Grosvenor Hotel, a half-timbered black-and-white building in the mock-Tudor style favoured by architects of the green and pleasant northern county. A telegram awaited our arrival and Holmes perused it with considerable satisfaction.

'Splendid, Watson! Another link in the chain!'

'Dare I ask the cause of your satisfaction?'

'My dear fellow, spare me that dog-in-the-manger expression! Feel free to see for yourself while I have a word with the head waiter before we eat.'

He tossed the cable to me, but I could make little sense of it. The message came from a property agent with an office in Liverpool's Castle Street, and simply confirmed that Mr Vernon Drake had sold Parkgate Hall some two-and-a-half years ago.

Over a late supper, Holmes regaled me with stories of cases which he had investigated in his youth, including the extraordinary affair of the barrister and the frog, which I hope one day he will set forth in writing. Of Meade the butler, however, he uttered not a word.

We breakfasted splendidly the next morning, whereupon Holmes asked me to accompany him to the principal sitting room for guests. He took a seat near the entrance that commanded a view of almost the entire hotel lobby. Although he feigned to peruse the morning papers whilst we each sipped a cup of Darjeeling, I was alert to the fact that he was waiting for a visitor to arrive.

As the clock struck ten, a veiled woman walked through the hotel door, and looked rapidly about her. Holmes sprang to his feet and stepped out of the sitting room to greet her. I followed a couple of paces behind.

'Miss Emma Drake?'

'Mr Holmes?' she whispered.

'Indeed.' My friend gestured towards me. 'This is my colleague, Dr Watson, and I beg you to speak in front of him with the utmost confidence.'

'Confidence,' the woman said slowly, 'is not a quality with which I am blessed.'

'Come, come, Miss Drake, I am bound to accuse you of false modesty. In my opinion, all that you have done requires a very great deal of confidence. Will you take a cup of tea with us? I can recommend the Darjeeling, the flavour is admirably full-bodied.'

Without waiting for a reply, he snapped his fingers for service, and waved Miss Drake into a chair. As the waiter approached our table, I studied the newcomer. She was neatly but inexpensively dressed, and her veil obscured features which appeared to be regular if unmemorable. Her fingernails were short and she wore no rings or other jewellery.

'Mr Holmes, I have responded to your advertisement in the *Chester Chronicle*, but I must confess that I am in no mood for social pleasantries. You stated in the advertisement that you had urgent information to impart concerning the fate of Mark Meade, who was formerly in my family's service.'

'Indeed I have. Meade has gone missing, much to the distress of his employer, Sir Greville Davidson.'

'I am sorry to hear it, but I cannot see that the matter is any concern of mine. Some time has passed since Meade was in my family's employ.' She made as if to rise from her chair. 'Your notice indicated that it was imperative I speak to you in person, yet I fail to see...'

'Bear with me, please,' Holmes said, lifting a hand. 'If I may be so bold, I doubt you have pressing engagements elsewhere, so I may crave your patience for a few minutes.'

'How would you know anything about my personal engage-ments?' the woman asked, her tone an odd blend of bitterness and curiosity.

'On making enquiries, I was sorry to learn that your ances-tral home, Parkgate Hall, was sold to defray debts incurred by your brother Vernon. He was excessively fond of gambling, as I understand, and excessively poor at choosing the right horse upon which to hazard a handsome sum.'

'When our mother and father died in quick succession, we were left with comfortably enough means to support our-selves,' the woman muttered. 'He was twenty-two and I was nineteen. We were never close while our parents were alive, and once Vernon had the freedom to do as he pleased, he became a libertine. Wine, women and wagering, he used to say, those were his priorities in life. As a matter of fact, he often dined here, sparing no expense.'

Holmes nodded. 'The head waiter remembers him well.'

'I dare say. My brother was lavish with gratuities, but the recipients of his *largesse* melted away when the money ceased to pour from his pocket. Within five years we were ruined.'

Holmes studied the woman intently. 'It must have been a very shocking experience. Tell me, what did you do?'

Emma Drake stared at him through the veil. 'I sought to earn a living, Mr Holmes, what choice would a destitute woman have?'

'That is the truth, if I may say so, Miss Drake, but not the whole truth,' Holmes said gently. 'But let that pass for the moment. It became apparent to me, when Sir Greville recounted his tale, that the butler Meade was a remarkable person.'

'I gave him a first class reference,' the woman said. 'There my obligations to him ended.'

Holmes raised his eyebrows. 'I read the reference, Miss Drake. I note that you gave your address as Parkgate Hall, which stands on the west side of the Wirral Peninsula, only a short drive from this very hotel. But I have received confirmation from a local agent that your brother sold the family home a year before you supplied the reference.'

The veil made it impossible to read the expression in Emma Drake's eyes, but from the way she shrank in her chair, I made sure that she was frightened. Holmes seemed to have calculated the effect of his words, and he continued his discourse in the same reasonable yet relentless manner.

'When Sir Greville first spoke to me, I found his account of Meade and the fellow's behaviour somewhat singular. A butler who is an accomplished pianist, and who disappears from view shortly after he is promised that he will receive a fortune? Extraordinary. As was his decision then to send a message of apology from Camden Town. What could it mean? I asked myself.'

'And what answer did you postulate?' Miss Drake asked coldly.

'Sir Greville dismissed the finding of certain bloodstained garments in the vicinity of his estate as irrelevant, but such an unusual incident and the strange behaviour of Meade were unlikely to be coincidental. The butler's personality intrigued me. Sir Greville is elderly and plainly grief-stricken following the death of his wife, but he is *compos mentis*, and I felt that only a remarkable individual could induce such a man to make a servant the beneficiary of the bulk of his not inconsiderable wealth.'

'Meade *is* a remarkable fellow,' the woman said in a soft voice.

Holmes lifted his eyebrows. 'The message Meade sent from Camden Town intrigued me. I surmised that it was intended to discourage Sir Greville from pursuing the butler, but also to lay a false trail, by implying that Meade was staying in London. I set some associates of mine the task of ascertaining from certain urchins of their acquaintance in Camden Town whether a particular person had been seen posting a letter at about the time when Meade's message had been sent. A long shot, frankly, but I was rewarded by my associates' assiduity – they were able to confirm a sighting that tallied with an embryonic theory of mine.'

I could not resist saying, 'You had sufficient data upon which to form the beginnings of a theory?'

'Most certainly, Watson. I found Sir Greville's account of Meade highly suggestive. There is no reason why a butler should not play the piano, but it is an accomplishment seldom manifested among those who make their living below stairs. Meade was a child in comparison to many butlers, and I wondered what had led him to move from this part of the world to the capital. What if Meade were not the man he seemed to be? Yet as soon as the question is posed, one is bound to speculate about the effusive testimonial provided by your good self, Miss Drake.'

'I have the highest regard for Meade,' Emma Drake said stiffly.

Holmes smiled. 'I asked myself what might have prompted the butler's sudden disappearance – could it have been the emergence of a person in possession of information to Meade's discredit? Or, perhaps, a person who knew that Meade was not what he seemed.'

Despite herself, Miss Drake was curious. 'What makes you so sure that he was not what he seemed?' she breathed.

'At first I was not sure. The idea that had begun to form in my mind seemed extraordinary. But a further conversation with my client was enough to convince me that the theory was sound. The handwriting of the reference from Miss Drake was obviously disguised – I presume that the left hand was used, rather than the right, but I detected one or two characteristics present in Meade's note to Sir Greville.'

I said, 'You mean that Miss Drake did not write the reference?'

'On the contrary, Watson.' Holmes smiled at my puzzlement. 'But it was a simple matter to deduce that Meade's first name was Mark.'

Miss Drake clutched at her throat. 'You know, don't you?'

'Certainly, I know that Mark Meade is an anagram of Emma Drake.'

'Holmes!' I exclaimed in bewilderment. 'What can this mean?'

'Why,' my friend said suavely, 'that Miss Emma Drake and Mark Meade the butler are one and the same person.'

I turned to the woman in horror. 'Miss Drake! Surely...'

She ripped the veil from her face. Her cheeks were ashen, her lips trembled, and yet there remained a quiet and impressive dignity about the woman, even at this dark moment. She lifted a small white hand.

'Yes, Doctor, Mr Holmes is correct. As soon as I read the advertisement in the newspaper, I feared that my secret was out. Everyone has heard of the brilliance of Mr Sherlock Holmes.'

My friend bowed. 'I take it that your decision to live as a man was dictated in part by financial necessity, but to a greater extent by personal choice?'

The woman inclined her head. 'Yes, you are right. I had no wish to earn a living as a maid, but I fancied that the life of a butler might prove rather agreeable. Throughout my youth, I had a fondness for dressing up as a boy, and often I borrowed my brother's clothes. Vernon always hated me – I think he was jealous from the moment I was born – and one day he caught me in his room. I had borrowed his clothes and was masquerading in front of a mirror as a young man. From that day he tormented me, constantly threatening to tell our parents. After they died, he kept me at his beck and call while he squandered his inheritance. At the time he sold the house to pay a fraction of what he owed to his creditors, I made my escape under cover of darkness, taking with me a wardrobe of male clothing which I had accumulated over the preceding months. I moved to London and started a new life, while remaining terrified that Vernon would one day track me down and expose my true identity.'

'You heard of Sir Greville's need for a butler and applied for the post?' Holmes said.

'Yes, and I must tell you that I have never been happier than in his service – and that of his dear wife, whose death was such a blow to him. There were moments when I thought he must suspect, and there is a maid who seemed to divine my secret, although Martha is a kind girl, and gave nothing away. Oaklands Hall is the most decent household, despite the suffering and sadness it has witnessed in recent years. It grieved me so to leave, but I had no choice.'

'Because your brother found you?'

'Yes. He had become destitute and spent the intervening years roaming the countryside, begging and stealing, but always hoping that one day he would trace me and find an opportunity for blackmail. By a grotesque stroke of ill fortune, he found his way to Oxfordshire, and spotted me in Wallingford, undertaking a small service for my master. He was not deceived by my wig and male attire, for he had seen me dressed as a man before, and expected that, left to my own devices, I would adopt the way of life that has long seemed most congenial to me. He threatened to reveal to Sir Greville the fact that Mark Meade was a woman in a butler's garb. I agreed to steal some items of jewellery from my late mistress's room and give them to Vernon on Saturday evening, but I knew such a crime was bound to be the first of many that he would force me to commit. I had perforce to flee, but I feared that, wherever I went, I would never rid myself of the anxiety that Vernon would discover me, and destroy my new life as he had destroyed the old.'

'So you murdered him?'

Emma Drake shivered. 'You make it sound so cold-blooded, Mr Holmes. I begged Vernon to set me free, but he laughed and said cruel and wicked things that I should sooner die than repeat, even to you. In my distress, I slapped his face and he responded by putting his hands around my throat. I wriggled free – he was never strong, and his dissolute way of life had further weakened his constitution. He chased after me, and I picked up a heavy stone that lay next to the ditch. Before I knew what I was doing, I dashed the stone against his temple. He fell to the ground and, God forgive me, I hit him again and again.' She half-stifled a sob. 'There was so much blood, Mr Holmes. I thought I should never be rid of it.'

'So, with Vernon's bloody rags abandoned in the ditch, and the body disposed of, you returned to Oaklands Hall and packed your belongings in order to leave forthwith?'

She nodded. 'I had committed fratricide. How could I stay, and inherit, after what I had done?'

'Especially,' Holmes remarked, 'when your brother's body, weighted down by the stone that killed him, reposed in the lake on the Oaklands estate.'

She stared at him. 'So you know everything?'

'Not quite,' my friend said, with a low chuckle that took me unawares. 'For instance, I am as yet unsure precisely how Mark Meade will explain his short absence to Sir Greville when he returns to resume his duties at the Hall this evening. I am, however, sure that this is a conundrum which will also soon be solved.'

She looked bewildered, as if unable to believe her ears. 'Mr Holmes, I... I don't know what to say.'

My friend waved a hand towards a Steinway piano on the far side of the sitting room. 'Do not trouble yourself with words, above all not with words of gratitude. You have rescued me from boredom, and thus I am in your debt, not *vice versa*. But the London train does not leave Chester for another hour. While we wait, would you care to indulge me for a few minutes with a little Chopin?'

Ann Cleeves

Mud

I was walking along the riverbank close to my home in the border town of Berwick, when the smell of the shore caught at the back of my throat and took me back forty years. Suddenly I was a schoolgirl again, on the bank of another estuary, in another small town in a rural county close to the sea. I'd walked along the Tweed many times before without the same experience, but perhaps not at this particular point in the tide or in the early summer. In any event what happened then was dramatic, a revelation. This was a Proust moment. The snapping of time. It was almost hallucinatory in its clarity. All at once I was a teenage girl, on my way to school, and the smell of inter-tidal mud provided the background to my dreams. My head was full of colour and romance and the sun was warm on the back of my neck.

I should have welcomed the magic that swept me back in time and allowed a few minutes to lose myself in the daydream. I should have found a quiet bench and sat there, a middle-aged woman smiling gently to herself. I should have breathed in that unique smell of salt and earth and rotting vegetation and remembered warm kisses, tunes played on cheap guitars, friends dressed in cheesecloth and denim. Instead I shut the memories out. I continued walking, picked up my pace and strode up the hill to the town. I got into my car and drove home.

But even here on the edge of a hill and miles from the river, the stink stays in my nostrils. I make a pot of strong coffee to dispel it, I drink strong red wine, but still the smell remains. Despite myself I sit in the dusk with the lights switched off and run the story of that summer in my head.

Every term time weekday I'd walk along the River Taw in North Devon to school. I'd get the bus from the coastal village where my father was the village headmaster into town and then stroll through the park to the Grammar School. The path is still there. I dropped in when I was in the region on business last year. But even then, with the river just yards away from me, I didn't have this experience, this vivid re-working of an old narrative.

Usually I made the walk alone, certainly in that year, at the end of my lower sixth. I had plenty of friends, but considered myself something of a poet and the solitary wander along the river was a statement, a signal to the others that I needed time alone to think. What poseurs we were! Sometimes the tide was full and with a westerly wind behind it the water was blown almost onto the footpath. Sometimes the river was hardly more than a trickle and the mud was baked in the sun. Then the salt marsh seemed to spread for miles right past the Long Bridge and out to the sea. It was marked by stranded small boats and the footprints of gulls and rats.

The sea played an important part in our social lives. Now Croyde and Woolacombe are famous as places to surf. Rich boys from London turn up with their fancy tents or they rent apartments in the big seafront houses and the roads are blocked by expensive cars. Everywhere you hear the loud, public school voices. When I was a girl the beaches belonged to us, to the kids who lived in the villages. At weekends and during holidays, we worked in the pubs and became waitresses and chambermaids, but the trippers, the grockels as we knew them, played no real part in our lives, except to stress how much we belonged. The visitors then came as families, and when the screaming children were dragged off to bed, we took over, skinny-dipping at midnight and building bonfires on the sand.

It seems to me now that we had more energy than anyone has a right to. We drank too much and read everything we could get our hands on, made music and sat for hours by firelight discussing love and friendship. We believed that nobody had felt so deeply. And into this mix came our leader, our guru, a small dark Northerner called Davie Raynor. *Mr* Raynor we knew him as, at first, because he was a teacher, a newly qualified teacher of Drama and English. But it became *Davie* when we were out of school because he was hardly older than we were. He lived in a flat on the coast not far from my home. Soon he turned up to our parties and sang Dylan with a guitar in his hands, sitting by the fire on the beach.

Towards the end of the school year, once exams were over, most of the lower sixth left to work in bars or hotels, but Davie Raynor had plans for our little group. He'd like to stage a production of The Caucasian Chalk Circle, he said. Brecht was a favourite. We'd have time to workshop it properly if we stayed on until the official end of term. Were we willing to do that? Of course we were. Even the boys were a little in love with him. He came from County Durham and his dad worked in a coalmine. He was strong and hard and none of us had ever met anyone like him before.

He held auditions at lunchtime in the school hall. There was a smell of rubber gym mat and floor polish. We pulled benches into a rough circle and he passed out scripts. He asked me to read for Grusha, the central character:

'Go on, Jen, give it a go.' Speaking in that strange, tight accent that set him apart.

I was considered one of the better actresses in our year, but I didn't think I had a chance. I knew where Davie's affections lay. He was besotted by Nell Pengelly, skinny, dark-eyed Nell with her long straight hair and her air of abstracted and silent concentration. He had never said anything about the infatuation, but he didn't have to. Occasionally I'd see him staring across a classroom at her and then forcing himself to look away. I knew he'd want Nell as his leading lady.

In fact he gave the part of Grusha to someone else entirely. Margaret Hill wasn't part of our group. Her father was a doctor and she lived in the town. She'd only remained in school after the exams because she didn't need the money that a holiday job would provide. Margaret was the sort of pupil that most teachers loved – she taught Sunday school, liked classical music and wore sensible shoes. She was captain of the house hockey team. God, how we despised her for all those things! Now

I think she must have been rather brave to stand against the flow of the tide, but there was something smug about her that would have irritated me even as an adult. It wasn't her common sense and responsibility but the unquenchable belief that she was always right.

So Margaret became Grusha and the rest of us took other parts. We lived and breathed the production. Even when we were away from school, we planned and rehearsed it. It must have been a magnificent summer for Mr Raynor. These articulate young people brimming with ideas and enthusiasm. And always, just on the edge of his vision, always in his mind, the beautiful Nell. A temptation and a thrilling possibility. Because she was aware of his admiration and the attraction was reciprocal. Nell was too passive to make the first move, but we knew that she'd respond if he approached her. As I said, we were all a little in love with Davie Raynor. During that long, dry summer it was as if the rest of us were holding our breaths, waiting for the drama to play out.

It happened after the dress rehearsal. We'd been working all day, painting details onto the set and printing the tickets, running through the songs. Mr Raynor was teaching and wasn't free until the end of school. As we ran through the production I saw how well it had all come together. Margaret was very good as Grusha, better than Nell or I would have been. She had an earthy, solid presence. We would have been too slight, too fey. We were performing in the round in the same hall where the auditions had been held. I sat on the floor, acting as prompt, though nobody forgot their lines that afternoon. We were showing off for Mr Raynor. The audience of parents and teachers on the following evenings would mean less to us than his approval.

Afterwards he offered Nell and me a lift home. Nell lived in my village. Her mother made pots in a shed at the end of their garden and her father was a writer of some sort. They'd only moved to North Devon three years before, but they were well accepted. We were accustomed to arty families moving in from outside. Davie stopped the car right outside our house. It was a school house, built in the playground. Tied accommodation, my father called it. We were saving for our own place, but teachers were paid very poorly in those days. I expected Davie to drive on to the cottage where Nell lived, but instead he turned to her.

'I'll walk you down, shall I?' he said. 'I could do with some exercise.'

Nell said nothing. She just nodded and followed him. I walked as slowly as I could across the yard, past the climbing frame where I'd played as a child, stopping every now and then to watch their progress down the lane. It was still light, but the shadows were very long and the sun was low over the sea. They seemed to be talking intensely and they walked just a little way apart, his stocky body and her slender one, moving almost in step. When I went to bed sometime later, his car was still parked outside our house.

On the bus to school the next day I asked her what had happened.

'Nothing,' she said. 'Nothing much. We talked.'

The younger kids on the bus were wired because it was the last week of term. The noise was ridiculous and stuff was being thrown, bags turned upside down, there were small scuffles. It was impossible to have a reasonable conversation. In town I pulled her with me to school along the path by the river, my arm in hers. The last thing I wanted that day was privacy. 'You have to tell me *everything*,' I said.

'Really,' she said, with her little smile. 'There's nothing to tell.'

'But he kissed you? He *must* have kissed you.'

'We have to be discreet.' Those weren't her words. I could hear Davie Raynor's flinty accent as she spoke them.

But they can't have been discreet enough because by the next day news of their relationship was common knowledge, in the sixth form common room at least. I don't know how it got out. I only told a few of my closest friends.

Margaret must have got word of it. I can see her now in the common room, a prefab hut furnished with cast-off easy chairs and scratched tables. She was making herself tea. Most of us drank coffee but she'd brought in her own teapot. Whenever I remember her she was on her own, surrounded it seemed by an invisible wall. The rest of us hugged and touched, but nobody went within two feet of her. She frowned as she stirred the pot and as she rinsed a mug under the tap.

'But they can't be going out together,' she said. 'He's a teacher. It's wrong.'

'Fancy him yourself, do you?' one of the boys shouted. His face was hidden by the NME he was reading and the words seemed to come from nowhere.

Suddenly Margaret blushed furiously and I saw that there was some truth in the suggestion. She dreamed about Davie Raynor at night. After all he'd chosen her, picked her out as his leading lady. And while we teased or ignored her, he was always gentle and courteous. Margaret didn't answer and the others were all too busy sniggering to notice her reaction. It would never occur to them that she might fancy anyone.

The play ran for three nights to full houses. It received a glowing review in the *North Devon Journal*. Margaret was marked out for special notice and I couldn't help feeling a stab of envy when I read the praise. Of course we'd planned a party for our final night. We were all aware that something special was coming to an end. The next academic year would be different; there would be A-levels and university interviews. We would make one more step towards growing up and becoming responsible, boring. We'd be constrained by the curriculum. But for a few more weeks we were free to be unruly in our ideas and our deeds. To drink too much cheap wine and believe that we would remain friends forever.

We chose Anchor Woods for the site of the party. On the south side of the estuary it was close enough to town for people who lived in the centre to walk home. I'd arranged to spend the night with a friend who lived close by. I don't know what plans Nell and Davie had made. We walked in a straggling, laughing gang across the timber yard and down the bank through the trees to the salt marsh, our bags clanking with the bottles we carried. The tide was out and there was driftwood to build a fire. Someone started to sing songs from Chalk Circle and we all joined in.

Davie sat next to Nell, his hand on her leg, all thought of discretion, it seemed, forgotten. In the firelight their faces glowed. Margaret was there too. Davie had insisted that we invite her:

'You can't leave her out, pet. She was the star. Besides, it's not fair to exclude her.'

And so I'd invited her, thinking that she'd refuse or that her parents, so strict and religious, would never agree to her attending, but somehow she'd wangled it because she was there, holding a plastic glass of Spanish white in both hands. It provided me with some amusement to think that she'd never drunk much before and that she'd probably throw up in her tidy, little girl's bedroom. What would her parents make of that?

Sometime later in the evening she wandered over and sat next to me. She still had a full glass of wine in her hands, but perhaps she'd been nursing the same one for most of the evening. Perhaps she was more sober than I was. It was hard to tell. She looked across the fire at Davie and Nell.

'It's wrong,' she said, frowning as she had in the common room. 'A betrayal of trust.'

'She's sixteen,' I said. 'Nearly seventeen. It's perfectly legal.'

'That's hardly the point.' She seemed suddenly horrified. 'So you think they're having sex? What if she gets pregnant?'

'Oh,' I said, sounding more wise and experienced than was actually the case. I had never got close to sleeping with a boy. 'I think they're both too sensible to let that happen, don't you?'

'It's wrong,' she said again. There was that stubborn insistence that she held the moral high ground. 'Someone should know.' She got to her feet as if she were about to stride off now to find a person in authority, the headmaster perhaps, to tell him that Nell Pengelly was being exploited by her teacher and that she needed rescuing. And perhaps at that point she did plan to rush home and surprise her parents with this interesting information. A gift to them to distract them from the fact that she'd been drinking, that her neat clothes were stained with marsh grass and bonfire ash. Her father was a school governor. He paraded with the teachers in his academic gown at speech day. I could see that this would end as a nightmare for Davie Raynor. He would be forced to leave the school and our life there the following year would be poorer and more boring.

'You can't do that,' I said quietly. 'Think about it. If Davie is forced out of his job everyone will work out who is to blame. Your life will be impossible.'

I saw at once that this was the wrong tack to take. Margaret would like to consider herself a martyr. It would please her to think that she'd sacrificed any popularity she might have had to save Nell Pengelly's soul. So my words just made her more stubborn.

The fire had died down now and it was quite dark. The only light came from the moon. In the shadows couples were sitting together, kissing, laughing. One pair was out on the mud, dancing very slowly to a tune that only they could hear. Margaret looked around her.

'It was a mistake to come,' she said. 'I'm going home.' She turned sharply and stumbled. It seemed she was a little drunk after all.

'You can't go on your own. You won't find your way through the trees without a torch.' Had I made my plan even then? Had I dreamed out the whole scenario in the seconds before the words left my mouth? Surely not. Sitting in my house on the hill, I convince myself that there *was* no plan, that what happened that night was all a dreadful mistake. 'I'll come with you,' I said. 'At least as far as the bridge. We can walk along the shore. But let's finish our drinks before we leave.'

She looked at the wine in her plastic glass and drank it in one go, wrinkling her nose as if it were medicine. Then I took her arm, as I'd taken Nell's on the path on the opposite bank of the river, and we walked quietly away. Nobody saw us leave. Everyone was too absorbed, too determined to squeeze the last drops of pleasure from the evening.

The tide was on the turn. Margaret was a town girl. She came to school along pavements, or more often her mother gave her a lift in her car. She didn't understand the river or the estuary as well as I did. And her last gulp of wine had tipped her into intoxication. She couldn't imagine the water seeping into the channels in the marsh, slipping like oil over the mud, covering the sand. She saw the lights of the Long Bridge in the distance and thought if she headed for those she'd be safe. Safer than scrambling through the trees of Anchor Wood in the dark. Her parents would have warned her about being out alone and the woods were close to a council estate, where unsuitable, even dangerous people might live. The moon over the mud seemed to mark a path for us to follow.

I went with her until she was almost there. 'Are you OK to go on now?' I asked.

'Of course.' She stood and looked at me. It was too dark to see her face, but in the way she stood she looked solid, unmoveable. 'I won't change my mind, you know. I'll tell my father about Mr Raynor. He'll know the next step to take.'

I shrugged. 'We all do what we have to do.' A slight breeze had come up, a westerly, pushing the tide ahead of it, bringing the smell of the sea inland to where we stood. The mud was already wetter under our feet. 'Take care,' I said. 'Are you sure you'll be OK?'

'Of course,' she said. And she stomped off, heading directly for the lights on the bridge, unaware of a deep gully, already filling, cutting into the mud. Soon the water would surround her and leave her stranded. If she'd sounded less certain, less sure of herself, perhaps I'd have called her back.

But I didn't. I made my way carefully back to the shore. When I was there I peered over the estuary, looking for a dark shadow, some evidence that she'd seen sense and moved to safer ground. A cloud covered the moon and I could see nothing. I shouted her name but there was no reply. I wandered back towards the party.

Someone had been scavenging along the shore and had pulled up a long piece of driftwood, white and smooth as bone, and had thrown it onto the fire. The flames danced again. Everyone was quiet now. There was no booze left. I approached the group with my arms full of wood too. I'd walked back through the trees, foraging as I went. They greeted me gratefully. Despite the mild night we'd be glad to keep the fire alight.

The cloud cleared briefly and we saw the moonlight reflected in the river. The tide was almost halfway full. Nobody missed Margaret. Nobody asked where she was. Soon after the party packed up. We retraced our steps. We went back to our ordinary lives. Lying on the floor in my friend's room, eventually I went to sleep.

Margaret's father phoned my parents early the next morning. In those days before mobile phones, communication was slower and I knew nothing about the call until I arrived home. My eyes were grainy through lack of sleep and my head ached. I was wearing the clothes I'd had on the night before and I hadn't bothered clearing off my make-up. I had what my father called 'panda eyes'.

'Dr Hill phoned.' My mother was easily impressed. She'd have loved being contacted by a doctor. 'He wondered if you knew where Margaret was. I hadn't realised you two girls were so close. Apparently she'd told her father that you were her best friend. That's why he rang here.'

'She was at the party,' I said. The idea that Margaret had considered me any kind of friend was astonishing. 'She left before I did.'

And that was the story I stuck to. Margaret had been at the party but only for a short while. It wasn't really her scene and she'd decided to go home. I'd offered to go with her but she'd said she'd be OK. I stuck to it even after the high September tides washed up her bloated body. And eventually I convinced myself that it was true.

The relationship between Davie and Nell didn't survive the summer. He decided he wasn't born to be a teacher after all and went off to make his fortune as an actor. I saw him once in an episode of a Northern soap on the television, but the close-up of his face didn't have the same affect as walking along the River Tweed today.

I sit in my house in the hills and watch the sky get light in the east. I still believe I can smell the mud.

Cath Staincliffe

Riviera

I never think of myself as a murderer. And it was never my idea. It was Geoffrey's from the get-go. She was his mother. It would never have happened if it had just been me. Does that sound feeble? I suppose I was – feeble – for long enough. But killing someone – well, that wasn't feeble.

At first it was just comments. Mutterings and murmurings about how Nora was an albatross round our necks and how she would live to get a telegram from the Queen just to spite him. I let it wash over me. Kept my own counsel. After the redundancy – that's when it changed. He began working out all these elaborate plans. I thought he was joking for long enough but then it wasn't funny anymore. Deadly serious.

Geoffrey's always been one for those forensic programmes on the telly. Normally he's a bit squeamish; he'd never watch an operation, say, and if he cuts himself shaving or even gets a spell in his finger from the garden he's all theatrical sighs and wincing and pale sweaty brow. He can't watch me quarter a chicken or clean a fish. But as long as there's a forensic side to it, something to do with crime and punishment, then he's happy as Larry; up to his eyeballs in blood and gore.

He turned to me one night after *CSI*, where they'd nailed this fella because he'd left dandruff at the murder scene, and he said, 'She'd have to disappear.'

I stopped knitting (I was doing a lovely matinee jacket for the girl next door who was due soon) and I stared at him.

'We'd have to get rid of the body … but we'd plan it first so that people expected her to go.'

I frowned. 'Like she was ill or something you mean?'

'No!' He sighed and put on his patience-of-a-saint expression. 'If she got ill and died we'd have to have a doctor and a post-mortem. The science these days–' He broke off with a snort and waved in the direction of the telly. 'People can *think* she's died but actually we'll have … disposed of her.' He wasn't smiling. I was waiting for a punchline – but it never came. 'So,' he pushed his recliner further upright and leant towards me, 'we start off telling people Nora's moved, gone to Filey–'

'She hates Filey.'

'Scarborough then, Whitby, wherever. Just concentrate, Pamela.'

He hates being interrupted.

'Then a bit later we say she's had a heart attack and died and she wanted her ashes scattering at sea.'

I laughed at that. It didn't sound like Nora. She was nervous of water. I remembered when Geoffrey and I were courting and he was still living at Nora's, the three of us had shared a holiday together. Torbay, the English Riviera. It was wonderful, the sun cracking the flags and the houses with palm trees and restaurants with lights outside and warm enough to eat *al fresco*. We even saw Max Bygraves, he had a big place up on the hills and we saw him in his Rolls; I think it was a Rolls but I've never been very good with cars.

Anyway Nora would spend all day on the beach building up to a dip, said she was waiting for the sun to warm the sea up. Then, when the beach was emptying and the water was still, she'd wade in until the water was up to her waist and stand there. Never went deeper, never got her shoulders wet.

Her brother had drowned when they were children. She told me that week in Devon, after dinner one night. Only time I heard her mention him. They lived up in Harpurhey, big family, nine of them in all. Harold, that was her little brother, he followed the bigger ones to the canal one day. They weren't allowed to go in, it was full of muck and rubbish and god-knows-what from the mills, but the lads would dare each other and the big 'uns would jump in until someone saw and chased them away.

Harold was larking about with a bit of old chain at the side and he just tripped. He sank like a stone. Only five. Those that could swim tried to find him while Nora watched from the bank. But he'd gone and they had to fetch his parents from the mill.

Nora had clamped her mouth tight then, when she was telling me, and wiped her eyes and smoothed the tablecloth and then started stacking the cups and saucers like she was at home. We used to talk a bit before Geoffrey and I got married, then it all changed.

'She can't swim,' I pointed out, 'she wouldn't want her ashes in the sea.'

'There wouldn't be any ashes, would there?' Geoffrey snapped.

I didn't want to listen to any more of his stupid fantasies so put my knitting away and stood up.

'We'd have to do it somewhere neutral, somewhere they'd never connect to us,' Geoffrey said, following me into the kitchen. 'Then dispose of... the evidence.'

'How?'

He looked a little uncomfortable. 'There are ways: quarries, dumps... easier if it's in smaller sections.'

I'd an image of Geoffrey with my rubber gloves and a freezer knife. I shook my head. 'And then what?'

'We'd be able to sort all this out,' he waved his hand round the kitchen. 'Settle her estate...'

Estate? A two-up two-down in Ladybarn and a life insurance policy. I told Geoffrey. 'Not without a death certificate, we wouldn't.'

And he thinks he's the clever one.

I really thought he'd seen sense after that. But then a few weeks later, when there was nothing on telly, he switched it off and came and sat next to me on the sofa. That was very odd. Well, both things were odd: the telly never went off, not before bed, and the sofa was my space really, he had his recliner. For a moment I thought he was going to tell me he'd met someone else or had cancer or something.

'Pamela,' he says, 'I've worked it all out.' And he launches into a big explanation. How we tell people that Nora is going to stay with us for a bit, that her nerves are bad, the house is getting too much for her, and then a few weeks later we tell them she's very low and talking about doing something silly and the doctor's worried. 'Then,' he says, 'we need to find a believable way for it to look like suicide. She's too frail to hang herself. And I don't see how we could get a bottle of paraceta-mol down her.'

He was right, she ate like a bird, you could hardly grind it into her food.

'Women usually do it in the bath,' I said, 'easier to clean up.'

He went white then. Combination of blood and nudity, I shouldn't wonder. Got up and stalked out.

I thought if I kept raising obstacles he'd give up.

Next thing we had a run of bills: car insurance, MOT, the water rates went up, the TV licence was due. Geoffrey spent hours at the dining room table, sifting through papers, stabbing at a calculator and sighing.

One day after lunch I tackled him. 'We could sell the house.'

'What?'

'We don't need a place this size any more. Somewhere smaller, it'd be more economical, easier to run.'

'This is our asset,' he blustered, like I'd suggested he sell his body.

'Well, maybe now's the time to use it.'

'It doesn't work like that.' Geoffrey always says this when he wants to stop you talking about something.

'It can do. If you'd only just think about it!' I knew I sounded shrill but it upset me. The way he never gave me any credit. I know I'm not well educated and I was never a manager or anything like that but I'm not stupid. Geoffrey thinks everyone who doesn't agree with him one hundred per cent is stupid. I reckon I'd beat him in a proper IQ test, anytime. It was like that with Nora, we all knew Nora was a bit slow, she could barely read and sometimes it took her a while to grasp some-thing new but she coped perfectly well. She'd raised Geoffrey on her own after his father died, and looked after him well and held a job as a machinist for over thirty years. She was still capable. But not according to Geoffrey.

'Or Nora could sell up and move in here,' I said.

'What?' He grimaced. 'We'd all go mad!'

'Why?'

'Her wittering on and her bloody Bingo, she'd fill the place with cats and fag ends. She's losing her marbles as it is…'

'She could have her own room. We could make it en suite.'

'En suite! She doesn't even know the meaning of the word.' He could be very vitriolic and it wasn't good for him; his face all red and spit in the corners of his mouth.

'So? She's not that bad. I wouldn't mind. It would sort the future out for all of us.'

'She'd ruin our lives and you know it. I can't think why you even raised it as a possibility. It won't be long till she needs constant care. Be a bloody nightmare.'

'Better than murder,' I muttered and left him to it.

I wouldn't care but it wasn't as if our position was desperate. Okay, there was no salary since his redundancy but if we budgeted really carefully we could manage on the interest from the savings plans he'd set up. The mortgage was paid off so it was only bills really. Granted there'd be no holidays and we'd have to keep an eye on the heating, perhaps trade the car in, but it was hardly as if we were going to be made homeless or go hungry.

I had one more go at him. Phyllis had told me about a scheme that she and Terry had signed up to when he had to go private for his op. In effect they'd sold their house to a building society but they could live in it for the rest of their lives. There was even provision for home nursing and the like. 'It's not as if we've anyone to pass it on to,' Phyllis said.

Same as me and Geoffrey: we never had children, just never happened. Phyllis and Terry had a boy, Jack, but he died as a toddler. Flu, would you believe. I think of that every time we have our jabs.

So, I tried telling Geoffrey about this scheme but he just pooh-poohed the whole thing. Said he didn't give a damn what suited Phyllis and Terry – they'd never had any business sense.

A week later Nora rang. She was in a bit of a tizzy and I couldn't get a clear story out of her. She rarely rang us up, though to hear Geoffrey talk about it you'd think she was onto us every five minutes. I didn't want to tell Geoffrey about it and get him on his hobby horse again so I told him I was going to walk down to the hairdresser's. I don't think Geoffrey would have noticed if I'd had my head shaved and had rude words tattooed on my skull, he's that unobservant.

Nora was upset because one of her cats had died. She'd had him fourteen years, not a bad innings. But she'd had a shock: tapped him to get him off the ironing board and he was rigid. She couldn't bring herself to put him out with the rubbish and she'd no garden, just a tub outside with a conifer in and she could hardly bury him in that. I told her I'd take him and put him in our border.

I made us some tea and we had a chat and she calmed down.

The place was a bit of a tip; everywhere thick with cat hairs and ashtrays full of cigarette ends but it wasn't dirty. The cats were trained and she still managed to clean out their trays often enough. She'd seven of them left. Not counting Elvis who was now wrapped in a thick bin liner, in a shopping bag by the front door.

We'd never been all that close, Nora and I. It wasn't really possible with Geoffrey daggers drawn. He'd made it clear once we were hitched that his mother was a cross to bear and the less we saw of her the better. But on the odd occasion that she and I got together it wasn't so bad, she was never funny with me. Geoffrey claimed you couldn't hold a decent conversation with her and that she was half-crazy but I never saw that.

Walking back up home I felt like I was carrying a weight with me – and I don't mean the cat. There we were, me and Geoffrey, big house, big car, big garden. Big and empty. No cats, no kids, not even a goldfish. Got me down, thinking that.

'Look at this.' He passed me a brochure. 'Palm Beach View. Paignton.'

'What's this?'

'A holiday,' he smiled. 'Good job you had your hair done.'

'We can't afford…'

'We can,' he had a funny look on his face, like he was building up to a surprise. 'Just a week.'

So we hadn't won the Lottery then.

'Me, you, my mother.'

'Nora!'

'She deserves a break.'

I realised then. My stomach went cold.

'Geoffrey…'

'Shh!' He put his fingers to his lips as if I were a child. 'It's all arranged.'

'But Nora – she might not want… there's her cats.'

'She'll go.'

And she did. He rang her up and told her to sort out someone to feed the animals. He was false jovial, if you get my drift. 'I want to treat the pair of you,' he said, 'you and Pamela. And besides there's a third off next week.' Which sounded more like it.

Nora probably thought I'd told him about Elvis and he wanted to cheer her up. As it was, he'd been out at the travel agents when I got back and I'd dug the creature a grave near the tea roses.

My stomach was upset so I just did omelettes that night. That was Tuesday. We were leaving on the Saturday. He kept quiet about it for the next day or two and I… well, I know it sounds pathetic but I was too frightened to ask.

Then he brings it up right in the middle of *Coronation Street*. He always does that, he knows it's the one programme I hate to miss. If I tried to breathe a word when he was watching one of his precious documentaries I'd soon know about it.

'It has to be an accident.'

'Geoffrey, I don't want to know.'

He stared at me then, over the top of his glasses. I felt close to tears and I knew that wouldn't impress him. I sniffed.

'Oh, pull yourself together,' he raised his voice. 'It's our only option.'

'No!'

'Pamela, I know what's best. Trust me.'

'I don't want to know.' I put my hands over my ears and closed my eyes. I felt him stride out of the room and slam the door.

'You look a bit peaky, love,' Nora said when we picked her up from home. 'Sea air'll do you the world of good.'

Geoffrey kept the radio on which saved us from having to make conversation. Now and again Nora would join in with some tune she liked, humming along, and Geoffrey would switch to another programme.

The guest house was very nice. 'Ooh, look!' Nora cried when she saw the view from her room: the sea a petrol blue and the headland sweeping round. Her eyes were shining. 'It's perfect,' she turned and smiled at me.

I could feel a headache coming on as I unpacked but I didn't like to lie down and leave the two of them on their own.

The Sunday we drove round the district. We had a seafood lunch in Shaldon and then Geoffrey drove us right up to Dartmoor, where we saw the ponies, and back along by the River Dart. All the time it was like I was holding my breath, waiting for something to happen. Nora noticed. That evening when we went down to dinner Geoffrey had forgotten his sweeteners and went back up to fetch them.

'Everything, all right?' she said. 'You don't seem so bright.'

I shrugged. 'Bit of a bad head.'

'This,' she nodded at our surroundings, she shook her head. 'Thank you.' She stretched out her hand and squeezed mine.

Oh, God. She thought it was my idea. That I'd wanted to treat her.

Monday we went up to Berry Head. It was fine weather, breezy on the top with blue skies, warm sunshine.

'Look at that,' Nora said, 'see halfway to France.'

'Have a stroll?' Geoffrey suggested.

I swallowed hard. There was a burning in my chest and my ears were buzzing.

'Lovely,' cooed Nora and she got out of the car.

I hesitated. 'My headache…'

'Nonsense,' Geoffrey said quickly, 'fresh air's just the job.'

The path was worn; the earth red like it is in Devon. White rocks were placed every few feet, to mark the path in poor weather. The shiny turf was dotted with daisies and clover. The cooler air carried the bitter tang of the grass and I fancied I could smell the brine from the sea. I caught the chirping sound of grasshoppers, saw one go flying off as we passed by. We don't get them round our way, not warm enough.

Geoffrey led the way, then me, then Nora. There were signs up: warning notices about the cliff and some sections were fenced off.

Eventually Geoffrey stopped and we followed suit. The three of us stood in a row looking out to sea. The land fell away only a yard or so in front of us.

Nora shielded her eyes and studied the horizon. I looked down at my shoes, I could feel my heart stuttering, missing a step. My mouth was dry. I glanced at Geoffrey and he winked (*winked*) at me.

'Look,' I said to Nora, my voice high, pointing away to my left, along the coast beyond her. And she turned to see.

I swung round and shoved with all my strength. I heard Nora cry out and I took a step forward to see the body bounce, once against the cliff side, then again on the jagged rocks and land, slumped like a puppet, where the waves broke against the slabs of stone.

'Geoffrey!' I screamed, moving forwards and going down on my knees. 'Geoffrey!' The wind took my screams and flung them to the gulls.

'Oh, God!' Nora gasped.

'He slipped.' I was shaking, tears pricked in my eyes. 'That rock,' I pointed to the smooth boulder. 'I tried to catch him.'

She nodded, 'I saw you move.'

'Too late. Ambulance.' I staggered to my feet. I pulled my mobile phone out of my handbag. 'We never should have come. He said he felt dizzy this morning.' I pressed 999. The coastguards were very quick.

I sold the house. Too big for me, like a pea in a biscuit tin. I was going to get a flat somewhere that would suit if I needed help in years to come. Then Nora admitted the stairs at hers were getting too much for her and she was wondering about a bungalow.

It was a programme on telly set me thinking. And we ended up here – the Spanish Riviera. Geoffrey's life insurance policy paid out more than enough. Turned out Nora had cashed hers in years back to make sure Geoffrey had everything he needed at school and could go to college.

We're tucked away on a little unmade road a few miles from the main drag. We've our own bit of beach out the back and the only other way to reach it is by sea. No one bothers – it's not even marked on the tourist maps. Nora's out there now, I can see her, cooling off, waist deep, fag in hand. The cats love it; basking in the sun and chasing lizards.

We've enough space for friends to visit, Phyllis and Terry are due on Sunday, and there's even Bingo, once a week, up in town. Bit of an ex-pat enclave, really.

I've given a lot of things up: knitting and cooking and cleaning. We've a girl comes in, nice girl.

I read and I swim and I sleep like a baby. Nora has a telly in her lounge, gets everything on satellite, but I don't miss it. I'm learning the language and I do a bit of voluntary work – English conversation with the local children – those that need a bit of extra coaching. Keeps me young.

My golden years, that's how I think of them. Ended up here by accident really. When I look in the mirror, I don't see a killer, just a few more wrinkles every day – and most of them are laughter lines.

Stuart Pawson

Sprouts

Hey-hey! How are you doing? Me? I'm fine. Or I would be if I were somewhere else, like Ipanema, and hadn't consumed enough sprouts in the last couple of days to float a battleship, but thanks for asking. Blame it on Jimmy Loose Screw. Jimmy is a kind soul who wouldn't see one of his own hurt, unless they deserved it, of course, but that was unlikely. Somehow he felt responsible for my dietary requirements, which was admirable, except that it was Christmas, the season of goodwill to fellow men, and yesterday about five tons of sprouts were delivered. As I was the only client in the slammer at the time, it looked as if those little green balls of vegetation would be a prominent feature on the menu for the next few days. Trouble was, they were no longer ball-shaped. More like disintegrating sponges, thanks to four hours on a low light, keeping them warm, as Jimmy told me, between breakfast and lunch. Personally, I'd have preferred a double portion of Grandma O'Donegan's secret recipe meatballs, with a helping of wasabi on the side, and maybe a light dusting of chilli powder, but it looked as if it would have to be sprouts for the foreseeable future.

'Eat them,' Jimmy said with a knowing inclination of his head, 'then you'll have something to tell the magistrate, show him how you're attempting to rehabilitate yourself.'

'By eating sprouts?' I enquired of him. I knew of several schemes and initiatives to help young cock-a-doodles through their formative years without them gathering too many bonus points in their passbooks, but none of them involved the consumption of large quantities of sprouts. Indeed, I'd been a star performer on many of those schemes and initiatives until a probation officer called Spiderman had a rubber stamp made that bore the solitary word *irredeemable*, which he used with gusto and red ink on any document he came across that bore my name, and I don't recall sprouts or any other vegetable ever being mentioned. Apart, that is, from the bananas and oranges that sometimes fell off the back of Italian Joe's cart when he made his deliveries. And apples. And maybe a few carrots or potatoes.

'Not just ordinary sprouts,' Jimmy told me. 'Them's holy sprouts.'

Now I had a good Christian upbringing, and although I wracked my brain for a good minute I could not recall any lines in the Bible, or any sermon I'd sat through, that included the word *sprout*. I brought this to Jimmy Loose Screw's attention, but instead of being grateful he assumed an aggressive posture and moved as if to take my sprouts away, or, worse still, to give me a double helping.

'Look,' he ordered, picking up one of the sprouts he'd brought with him, and stabbing at it with his fingerless-gloved index finger. 'See? There's a cross on the bottom. That's a Christian symbol.'

I held his wrist steady and pulled his hand towards my face. He was right – there was a cross cut into the end of the stalk. I checked a few of the new ones, and they all bore a cross.

'Hey-hey,' I said. And: 'Well-well.' And: 'Who'd have thought it?'

'So what are you going to do about it?'

I wasn't going to do anything about it. I'm not the type of fellow who complains about this and that as if everything could be put right with a few sharp words. Words never boiled a kettle of fish, as my old Mama, God bless her, loved to remind us. If it's not a serious issue, let it go, but if it's more personal, like them bad-mouthing your lady, or using your pool cue, more drastic action is called for. Something like that could deserve a good whacking. 'I'll eat a few,' I told Jimmy, 'but I can't manage them all.'

'I meant on Monday. What are you going to tell the beak?'

'Thank you for reminding me, James,' I said. 'Otherwise it might have slipped my mind. At this moment I haven't thought out a strategy, but perhaps that is something you, with your vast experience in matters of a legal nature, could help me with.' Adding, as an afterthought: 'Who, as a matter of interest, is the beak on Monday?'

'The Reverend Herod.'

Jeez, I thought. Sprouts and Herod on the same day. He wasn't always called Herod. Word on the streets, which could usually be trusted, except when the ponies were running, was that he changed his name so that it fell more in line with his political views. What was certain was that he once advocated judicial drowning of the first born of every household on the Seacroft estate. Personally speaking, I thought it was a good idea. When the ponies were running you didn't believe nobody. Not even your maiden aunt who's making out with one of the jockeys. Especially her. When you are playing the pony game there is no substitute for knowing all about horses. You watch them parade; listen to what your lady-friend's hormones tell her; look to see if its ears are pricked and count its legs. Sometimes, when you consider all that, one horse stands out from the rest. That's the one you put a few spondulicks on. Me? Hey-hey, though I say it myself I do have something of a gift for picking winners. Well, if not winners, then triers.

'So what will you say?' Jimmy asked me.

'I don't know,' I told him. 'You may have noticed that sometimes I am lost for the right phrase or expression. I am not as articulate as I would like to be, then I could put my case forward in a way that would show me in a good light. As things are, I find myself stumbling over words and I am afraid that my natural reticence will be misinterpreted by the good Reverend, which could work against me.'

'You could have fooled me,' Jimmy Loose Screw said.

'So what would you do?'

'I'd work out what I wanted to say, then say it.'

'But I forget what I want to say. Sometimes I'm a bit lacking in the old memory department.'

'Then write it down, Snozzletoft.'

'Hey-hey, that's good. Write it down. Why didn't I think of that? How do you spell *robbed* and *bank*?'

'I thought you didn't do it.'

'*I didn't.*'

'Well then, I'm only trying to help.' 'Enjoy,' he added as he turned to leave.

I studied the congealing gravy, the lone potato and the mountain of sprouts he'd left for me and decided that he, Jimmy Loose Screw, was right. I'd be foolish – nay, suicidal – to give in without a fight. I pushed the plate away and shouted after his echoing footfalls: '*Jimmy*,' I yelled. 'Jimminy, my old buddy. *Jimmy!* Don't desert me in my darkest hour. I'm a reformed character. I'll be a good person. I'll go to mass, if it's not raining. And I promise not to have lewd thoughts when Mrs Boccolinsky leans over to find the best tomatoes at the front of her counter. So Jimmy, can you hear me? Be a good schmucker and bring me a pencil and some paper. *Please.*'

Philip Iqbal, I learned, had only worked at the bank for three months, and never behind the counter. But half the staff were absent due to the flu epidemic, the manager told him, and it would be a great help to all concerned: the staff still at work; the public; young Philip himself and senior management who would be made aware of his contribution – if he could step into the breach on this, one of the busiest days of the year.

Philip, who aspired to be a manager himself, thought about it, liked the bit about it appearing on his career development chart and said OK, he'd do it. The manager heaved a sigh of relief and started a crash course on *How to be a Bank Teller* in one easy lesson.

An hour later, content he'd covered all eventualities and eager to return to the sanctuary of his centrally heated office, the manager screwed the top on his Mont Blanc fountain pen and said: 'Good lad. I think that's about everything. Do you have any questions for me?'

Philip, ambitious and programmed to absorb knowledge, did have a question. He said: 'Yes sir. Just one.'

'Oh, fire away.'

'Well, sir, what do I do if a bank robber comes to my counter and sticks me up?'

In twenty-two years of banking the manager had never witnessed a stick-up. 'That's a good question,' he said, mind racing to remember company policy. In a few seconds it came to him and he dived under the counter. 'You give the robber this,' he said as he resurfaced clutching a dusty manilla envelope. 'No heroics, just hand it over. There's two thousand spondulicks inside, marked with invisible ink. Just give it to him.'

'Oh, right, thank you, sir,' he said, then, into his microphone: 'Next customer to position seven, please.'

Gaspipe felt the reassuring fold of notes in his jean's pocket and smiled. It was nearly a full week's pancrack but it would give young Kayleigh a start in life that he, Jason Atkinson, known as Gaspipe since an unfortunate accident with a lead pipe he was trying to relocate, had never had. Kayleigh was not quite three years old, but, come Boxing Day, he'd be tearing round the concrete corridors of the project housing block, laying the foundations of a career that could take him to the four corners of the world. Start early, that was the secret.

Look at Sideways Sid Montana: started in go-carts when he was four; now World Champion. Or Dean Johnson, known as Rocket Man, driving on daddy's homemade track before he could walk properly. A week's pancrack was a small price to pay to join such illustrious company. The battery-propelled Acemaker replica Ferrari would give young Kayleigh a foothold on the first rung of the ladder. Kayleigh's mother, Moonbeam, had resisted at first, but Gaspipe had talked her round. It would mean sacrifices, but dreams always carried a price tag. The price of this one was her own Christmas present and all the other treats normally associated with the festivities. She'd smiled wryly and kissed goodbye to the genuine leather Spanish boots she'd been coveting. Gaspipe counted his money again and headed into town.

Gaspipe didn't go into town very often, so much of it was new to him. He'd never been to the Apollo Discount Centre; only perused their monumental slab of a catalogue out of boredom when they were between TV sets. That's where he'd seen the replica Ferrari which he was about to collect, having reserved the last one in stock by telephone. The Apollo shop wasn't where he thought it would be. In truth, the street on which the Apollo stood wasn't where he thought it would be, usurped by a flyover and a modest office block which proclaimed itself as United Fiscal Solutions. He pulled up the hood of his FCUK top and circumnavigated the block until he saw the sign for the Precocious Child pub, scene of much of his growing up and where he'd met Moonbeam, four years previously. And that was his undoing.

Just one, he thought. Just one. He deserved it. He fingered the wad of money and did the calculation. He had three spondulicks more than the cost of the car; enough, he reckoned, for a pint of Bishop's Finger. He thrust his way into the steamy innards of the bar and placed his order.

That first long, lingering sip slid down his throat as effortlessly as children sliding down the chute at a waterpark. He was vaguely aware of the landlord placing his change on the bar between them as he came up for air and dived straight into his second long draught.

His change from the fiver he'd paid with was one-ninety. When he queried it with the landlord he was told it was correct: Bishop's Finger was three-ten a pint. 'I didn't order a sandwich with it,' he protested, but the landlord was unmoved. Blame it on the high rent, he told Gaspipe. Blame it on the Government's taxes. Blame it on the smoking ban and the drink-driving laws. Blame it on everyone except him. And it was still three-ten a pint.

Gaspipe drained his glass and wandered towards the city centre, where the hustle and bustle, the beeping of cash machines and the rattle of charity collection boxes created the illusion of easy living and goodwill to all men. He bought a newspaper that he knew would have that day's race card in it and found a bench where he could sit and study form.

All he needed was a quick winner at any price. The odds-on favourite at Dogberry Park looked a likely candidate so he put one spondulick on it, earning himself a sarcastic comment about big spenders from the sheepskin-coated bookmaker. The horse finished seventh in a field of eight. He now needed a winner at slightly longer odds.

It didn't come in the next four races. His betting gradually became more reckless as he tried to recompense his losses until, with one final desperate gamble that would have enabled him to stroll into the Apollo Centre and buy the Acemaker battery-operated Ferrari, he blew the lot in.

He found another bench to sit on and pondered the situation. To his left an old man was blowing into a tin whistle, repeating the same three notes over and over. To his right a close harmony group dressed in some South American ethnic costume were sending the workers back to their desks to the tune of Mary's Boy Child. Directly in front of him was the head branch of the Royal City Bank. A flurry of snow came tunnelling down the precinct and the whole city shivered. His problem was simple: he needed a hundred spondulicks and he needed them fast. What Moonbeam would do to him if he returned home empty handed and penniless brought tears to his eyes. He clambered to his feet and set off towards the outdoor vegetable market with a renewed determination in his stride, pausing only to deposit the newspaper in a litterbin.

Young Philip Iqbal enjoyed meeting the public. It was the festive season, and most of the transactions were withdrawals, but he checked balances, transferred monies, paid bills and deposited cheques. But mainly it was withdrawals. He did it all with the courtesy and efficiency that were his birthright, basking in largess as he handed over bundles of cash to grateful customers and returned their Merry Christmases.

The note read: I have a gun. Give me some money or I'll blow your brains out.

'I beg your pardon?' Philip wondered.

This time his assailant spoke. 'I have a gun. Give me some money or I'll blow your brains out.' The paper bag he laid on the counter certainly looked as if it might contain a gun.

Philip hesitated for a few seconds as he recalled his brief training session. Don't be a hero, he remembered. Hand over the money and don't be a hero. 'Oh!' he exclaimed, reaching under the counter to retrieve the manilla envelope. 'This is for you,' he said, manoeuvring it under the reinforced glass partition, into Gaspipe's eagerly awaiting hands.

Gaspipe couldn't believe his luck. He grabbed the envelope and ran for the exit.

A private hire taxi from the other company – the one they didn't use for the weekly supermarket run – as ordered by him five minutes earlier, was standing at the kerb, engine running. Gaspipe yanked the passenger's door open and flopped into the comfortably worn seat of the elderly Mercedes, saying: 'Middleton, please. Acre Road,' as he looked back at the bank.

'Are you Mr Zermansky?' the taxi driver asked.

'Er, no, I'm Mr Smith. I rang for you a few minutes ago.'

'Sorry, pal, not me. I'm looking for Mr Zermansky.'

'What difference does it make? He can go in my taxi.'

'It's bad for our reputation if we don't turn up. I'm afraid you'll have to get out, Mr Smith. Your ride should be along in a few seconds.' Jason Gaspipe, aka Mr Smith, looked back at the bank again. People were spilling out onto the pavement, staff and customers alike, some brandishing camera phones and pointing. Jason stuffed the manilla envelope into the glovebox of the Merc and opened the door. He could hear the siren of a police car, very faint but growing louder.

Full stop, the end. Hey-hey, that's it. I've done it, just like Jimmy Loose Screw said I should. And a ho-ho too, for the season. It was harder than I thought, but worthwhile deeds don't grow on banana trees, as Mama, God bless her, used to say.

Apparently it was this zonco, known as Gaspipe according to one witness, who did for me. I only knew him as Mr Smith, but try telling that to a judge. He had form for burning down the polytechnic, but arsonists don't usually transmogrify into bank robbers, according to the probation officer who knew him, so they weren't taking that information with the seriousness I deemed it worthy of. And it was doubtful in law if a cucumber in a paper bag counted as armed robbery. I'd bet my last coppers it was Spiderman who pointed the poisoned chalice at me, but what does a humble taxi driver know?

I sat there watching the action in my rear-view mirror, enjoying the excitement of the blue lights getting closer, the siren notes rising and falling, the snow beginning to swirl as if part of the scene's orchestration, safe in the knowledge that it was nothing to do with me, warmed by the righteous feeling that all that was in the past.

At some time during this reverie, Gaspipe legged it.

Jimmy Loose Screw just came in, to see if I was ready.

'Could you give these to the clerk of the court?' I asked, handing him my statement, and he said he would.

'I don't suppose there's a chance the good Judge Herod slipped on the icy court steps and broke his leg?' I ventured.

'Sorry boss, but there's been a thaw.'

'Curses,' I said. 'Curses and damnation.' I don't usually blaspheme, but I felt this little outburst was justified. 'What sort of mood is he in?'

'Well, he just fined someone a hundred spondulicks for not having a dog license.'

'We haven't had dog licenses for ten years.'

'They haven't had a dog for five.'

'That bad, eh? Do you think I'll go down?'

'For stealing two thousand big ones? I'd rather bet on the *Titanic* finally making it.'

'But I didn't do it.'

'The package they found in your glovebox says you did. Shall I take it you'll be staying for dinner?'

I gave a sigh that started right down in my boots and popped out of the top of my head. 'Yeah, I suppose so.'

'I'll make you a reservation.'

'Thank you. And what delicacies might there be on this evening's menu?' I asked.

Jimmy Loose Screw gave me one of those devilish grins that only those truly contented with their life's calling can conjure up.

'Take a wild guess,' he said.

InDex

(Being an extract from a draft index to *Celebrity Lawyer*, the autobiography of Jude Wykeham)

Wykeham, Jude

Affair
    With Esther Yallop
Autobiography
  Mysterious disappearance of
  Paid enormous sum to write
  Posthumous publication, anticipated
Guilt
    Presumed motive for suicide
Launch Party
  Meets Esther Yallop at
Police investigation of
  Errors in
    Fake suicide note, misled by
Publisher
  Shared with Esther Yallop
Puerto Banus,
  Purchase of holiday home at
  Weekends spent with Esther Yallop in
Queen's Counsel
  High earnings as
  Rhetorical skills
  Seduction, persistent employment of when engaged in
  Strangling
    Suspected of
  Suicide
    Apparent

Yallop, Esther

    Dress
      Expensive tastes in
      Provocative
    Erotic poems
      Authorship of
      Lover, dedicated to
    Husband, boredom with
    Sarcasm, gift for
    Strangulation of
      Pleasure taken in
        Remorse for, subsequent

Yallop, William
    English degree, uselessness of
  Indexer, part-time employment as
  Manuscript
    Re-writing of
    Theft of
  Novels, unpublished
    Personality
  Despair, tendency to
          Obsessive
    Revenge, lust for
  Writing,
  Career, literary
        Experimental nature of
     Failure in
  Celebrity Lawyer, determination to compile index for
  Confession
      Double murder, to
        Index, by means of

Murder Squad
Author Biographies

ANN CLEEVES has been published for twenty-five years. She's best known for her Shetland Quartet and her Vera Stanhope series. *Raven Black*, the first of the Shetland novels, won the CWA Duncan Lawrie (Gold) Dagger for 2006. It was later adapted for Radio 4's Saturday play and *White Nights*, the second in the series, will be broadcast later this year. The Vera Stanhope books have been adapted for a major ITV drama starring Brenda Blethyn. Ann lives in North Tyneside with her husband.

MARTIN EDWARDS' latest Lake District Mystery, featuring DCI Hannah Scarlett and Daniel Kind, is *The Hanging Wood*, published in 2011. Earlier books in the series are *The Coffin Trail* (shortlisted for the Theakston's prize for best British crime novel of 2006), *The Cipher Garden*, *The Arsenic Labyrinth* (shortlisted for the Lakeland Book of the Year award in 2008) and *The Serpent Pool*. He has written eight novels about lawyer Harry Devlin, the first of which, *All the Lonely People*, was shortlisted for the CWA John Creasey Memorial Dagger. In addition he has written a stand-alone novel of psychological suspense, *Take My Breath Away*, a novel featuring Dr Crippen, *Dancing for the Hangman*, and completed Bill Knox's last book, *The Lazarus Widow*. He has published a collection of short stories, *Where Do You Find Your Ideas? and other stories*; 'Test Drive' was short-listed for the CWA Short Story Dagger in 2006, while 'The Bookbinder's Apprentice' won the same Dagger in 2008. He has edited twenty anthologies and published eight non-fiction books, including a study of homicide investigation, *Urge to Kill*. His website is www.martinedwardsbooks.com and his blog www.doyouwriteunderyourownname.blogspot.com

MARGARET MURPHY is the author of nine internationally acclaimed psychological thrillers — both stand-alone and police series. Her work has been shortlisted for the First Blood award and the Crime Writers' Association (CWA) Dagger in the Library. Her short fiction is featured in *Best British Mysteries 2006* and *The Mammoth Book of Best British Crime* (2009). She is the founder of Murder Squad, a monstrously talented and thrillingly diverse bunch of writers who have supported, sustained and enriched her life over the last ten years. She has chaired the CWA Debut Dagger competition for unpublished writers and is a former Chair of the Crime Writers' Association. She is proud to have held a Royal Literary Fund Writing Fellowship from 2008–2011. Her website is: www.margaretmurphy.co.uk

STUART PAWSON is creator of Detective Inspector Charlie Priest — once the youngest inspector in the East Pennine force, and now its longest-serving inspector. He has recently enjoyed his thirteenth outing in the fictitious Yorkshire town of Heckley, situated in what was once called the Heavy Woollen District. Stuart's first career was as an engineer in the mining industry but this came to an end with the demise of coalmining. He followed this by working part-time for the probation service for five years. His chief hobbies have been oil painting and fell walking and he has incorporated these in the character of Charlie Priest. Stuart and his wife, Doreen, live in Fairburn, Yorkshire, with no cats, just four lusty tortoises.

CATH STAINCLIFFE is an established novelist, radio playwright and the creator of ITV's hit series *Blue Murder,* starring Caroline Quentin as DCI Janine Lewis. Cath's books have been shortlisted for the Crime Writers Association Best First Novel award and for the Dagger in the Library and selected as Le Masque de l'Année. *Looking For Trouble* launched private eye Sal Kilkenny, a single parent struggling to juggle work and home, onto Manchester's mean streets. *Missing* is the seventh and latest title. *Trio*, a stand-alone novel, moved away from crime to explore adoption and growing up in the 1960s, inspired by Cath's own experience. Cath's newest novels, *The*

Kindest Thing and *Witness*, examine hot topical issues and tell stories of ordinary people, caught up in the criminal justice system, who face difficult and dangerous choices. Cath lives in Manchester with her partner and their children.

Visit our website and discover thousands of other
History Press books.

www.thehistorypress.co.uk